BREAKING POINT

By

C T Mitchell

Copyright (2nd Edition)

Copyright © 2020 by C T Mitchell
Cover and internal design © Wood Duck Media

All rights reserved. No part of this book may be reproduced
in any form or by any electronic or mechanical means, including
information storage and retrieval systems, except in the case of
brief quotations in articles or reviews, without the permission
in writing from its publisher, C T Mitchell.

All brand names and product names used in this book are
trademarks, registered trademarks, or trade names of
their respective holders. We are not associated with
any product or vendor in this book.

FREE Downloads

Build your C T Mitchell Library with two free downloads
Over 100,000+ downloads to date.

Dead Shot
Murder at the Manor

www.CTMitchellBooks.com

TABLE OF CONTENTS

CHAPTER 1

"He doesn't smell like grilled chicken, does he, sir?" the young constable said with a smug smile to Detective Jack Creed, who was crouched next to the charred remains of a body, the left wrist handcuffed to the downpipe under the kitchen sink. Creed seethed at the comment as it washed over him, giving the constable the death stare before he spoke.

"You make a comment to me like that again, Constable, and I'll have your badge and personally boot you off the force. Understand me?"

"I-I didn't—" the constable replied in a dry voice, his face ashen as Jack cut in and ordered the constable out of his sight.

"Tell Detective Pratt to finish up his interviews and meet me at the car. We're heading back to the station."

****

1

Detective Jack Creed looked at the dead bodies pinned to a wall in the incident room. There was a similarity. They were all black, mostly aboriginal. Their faces screamed innocence. Nobody was over 25. The first victim was murdered around 10 years ago. The last was found about eight months ago, doused in acid and the skin peeled off his body.

Creed was brought in to oversee the case. All the murders had occurred in and around Cabarita Beach, a sleepy seaside village in northern New South Wales, Australia. Mostly famous for surfing and fishing, the town was building a reputation as the 'murder capital of the northern coast.' The local constable was used to dealing with an occasional drunk at the Beach Hotel, but murder was not his expertise. Enter Detective Jack Creed, a no-nonsense copper from the school of hard knocks whose unorthodox methods annoyed the hierarchy but got results.

When Creed began on the case from his Kingscliff Police Station base, about a 20-minute drive from Cabarita Beach, he had nothing. Piece by piece he methodically put the puzzle together. The only missing part was the killer, but Creed's tenacity would ensure that one day either he or she would be caught. That was a given. Sooner or later the perpetrator would slip up. They always do.

Creed had four other victims from unsolved crimes. It appeared that they had all been killed by the same person but to date there were no clues that tied them all together. Operation Charlie, named after the first victim, was proving to be Creed's longest running case. Creed didn't like long cases. Normally he could wrap things up in few days, weeks at the latest. But this case was different. The only thing he and the profilers could be certain about was that there would be more.

The time between each murder meant the media had not caught onto the possibility that maybe Cabarita Beach had a serial killer living in its midst. That was a good thing, as the local press boys could whip up a whole bunch of hysteria; something he didn't need nor would the local mayor approve. The mayor was regularly on television promoting the area as the fishing capital of the world. The last thing the local hoteliers needed was the media saying there was a nutter running around the town killing people every 18 months or so. The vacancy rates would soar and Creed knew that somehow, he would be blamed for the empty beds.

Creed was also pleased that nobody else had cottoned onto the fact that all the victims were dark. If they did, then racial tensions would be rising. The police had been handing out warnings to young people for years not to stay out all night clubbing. Even though the night life in Cabarita Beach was bustling, the kids didn't heed any the police warnings anyway.

Creed thumbed through the files of missing people. A photo caught his eye. Tom Langley. He was older than the rest. Wrinkles exposed his hard life. Creed pulled the photo and put it to one side as he looked at the expressionless faces of other missing adolescent aboriginal kids.

"He doesn't fit the bill, Jack," Detective Sergeant Pratt interrupted. "He's too bloody old."

"Yep, that's why he's out of the file, Pratt," Creed replied without lifting his eyes from the folder. The operation had mainly focused on a broad area from Pottsville in the south, Lismore in the west and north to the Tweed. Creed thought of it as his 'Bermuda Triangle' where instead of boats or planes going missing, people disappeared here at regular intervals.

"Oh, by the way, Simpson has been taken to hospital. Heart issues. He might be out for a while," Pratt advised Creed.

"Shit. That's all we fuckin' need. Get a replacement and quick. I don't want that O'Halloran prick closing the case." Creed grimaced. They were making progress and the families could get closure soon.

Pratt returned an hour later with just three names and their profiles. "Sorry, mate, not a lot of choice out there."

Creed looked over the meagre pickings. The first guy was from Queensland, looking for a transfer to a 'quieter area.' Creed shook his head, amazed at the idiocy of some people. He definitely didn't fit Creed's mantra of working a case, no matter what it took, until it was solved.

Creed recognized the next name. Sergeant Peter Tebbitt and Creed worked briefly at Tweed Heads. Briefly being the operative word. Creed couldn't stand the guy, a self-centered, lazy arsehole. That left just one folder. And immediately there was a problem.

Detective Sergeant Joanne Boston-Wright grew up in the area. Her family resided just outside Bangalow. She had graduated with honors from the Academy, spent her probationary period in the back streets of Kings Cross before being transferred up to Lismore. Her file read "takes initiative," an ingredient Creed could use right now.

Boston-Wright, out of the process of elimination, was now the number one contender to be the new member of 'Operation Charlie.' She had been exposed to drugs, prostitutes, robberies and auto theft. Murder was about to be added to her resume, something she had previously tried to join but was knocked back. Murder is a bit of a boys club and Creed was a stickler for keeping the tradition, but he was desperate. He could maybe handle the fact that she was a woman, but a hyphenated surname? Would she be bringing her toffee-nosed, small 'L' liberal ideologies into the team? Would it mean the boys would have to curb the use of their favourite four letter word?

Creed was weakening. More to the point, he was desperate. Yes, she had an impressive resume, but Creed took those with a pinch of salt. "Never read a bad referral" was Jack's mantra, so why have them in the first place he would often say. What he needed was initiative. Somebody who could think on their feet but follow orders at the same time. Well, to be frank, Creed's orders. Creed wasn't the most order-abiding policeman on the force, something that had held his promotional prospects back.

Creed read the last paragraph of her CV. Jo was the daughter of Bruno Boston, a half Italian, half Aussie detective who not only developed Creed's love for Italian loafers, but was his first true mentor.

Pratt strolled in. "Any luck, Jack?"

"Give Boston-Wright a call. Get her on the team," Creed replied, slipping his Versace jacket on to add style to his Boss jeans.

"But she's got no form, Jack. We need somebody with experience in murder."

"At the moment, Detective Pratt, we need some different thinking. More importantly, we need more legs on the team to find our killer before that Irish mother fucker O'Halloran shuts us down. Would you like to go back to traffic?"

Creed slipped out of his office and Greg Pratt started dialing.

****

Boston-Wright was excited to have received her call. After all her years of hard training she was finally being called upon to do what she had joined the police force for – some hard crime solving. Too nervous to eat breakfast, Boston-Wright quickly knocked back a flat white coffee, jumped into her car and raced off to the Kingscliff Station, about 30 minutes from her home.

There she met Greg Pratt, a round-faced red-cheeked, heart-attack-waiting-to-happen kind of guy, along with Constable Singh, a light-framed, 30 something officer of Indian descent. The boys ushered Boston-Wright into the back seat of a panda car and sped off to 17 Cypress Avenue, Cabarita Beach, scene of the latest victim's burnt remains.

They parked the squad car about 200 hundred meters from the house. The rubberneckers were still commanding front row seats near the police tape. Some looked like they hadn't been home since yesterday. Boston-Wright followed Pratt and Singh up the street, giving the occasional sideways glance to the gawking onlookers. Why on earth would people loiter around such a gruesome crime scene? Did they really expect to see the blackened remains of the poor soul?

Pratt and Singh made a beeline to the mobile espresso van. Obviously some opportunist with an entrepreneurial flare decided that Cypress Avenue could be a good spot to set up shop for a few days to feed the hungry troops investigating the case. Pratt and Singh would not disappoint and promptly placed their orders for coffee and two ham with cheese croissants.

Boston-Wright was amazed at the lack of respect the boys were showing for the victim. "Shouldn't we go into the house?" she enquired, receiving a rookie look from Detective Pratt.

"I'm guessing you've already eaten then," Pratt responded while Singh chimed in with, "a decaf latte and muesli – organic, of course." Boston-Wright knew straight up she had a fight on her hands. Once again, she would need to prove herself in this male dominated industry, more so at the Kingscliff Police Station.

The boys devoured their breakfast as if it were their last meal. Tossing their polystyrene cups into the bin provided by the coffee van, they marched into the yard of the property and ascended the stairs two at a time. Looking at Pratt's broad arse, at least two axe picks wide, wobbling up the stairs in front of her, Boston-Wright couldn't help but wonder if that heart attack might come sooner than later.

"You lot took your time," Creed barked while inhaling a cigarette. Creed wasn't a big smoker, not since lung cancer claimed his brother four years ago, but he had the occasional puff around crime scenes. The smokes helped settle his mind and gave him time to think.

"Sorry, boss. Singh was feeling peckish," Pratt replied, dumping his junior offside right in Creed's bad books.

"You're our replacement?" Creed said looking directly at Boston-Wright with his piercing hazel eyes.

"I knew your father. A good bloke."

Detective Bruno Boston, known as 'The Don,' passed away 12 months ago from pancreatic cancer, the downside of living the good life of too much salami and vino. Boston-Wright always looked up to him, appreciated his guidance as she made her way through the ranks. She was now in the big league and would call upon her memory bank to harness the good advice her father had passed on. Above all else, she wanted to uphold the Boston name and be as good a copper as Bruno. As for Wright? Well that's another story. The divorced Jo knew there wasn't much she needed to do to better herself than being with that low mongrel. Brett Wright had trouble keeping his willy inside his pants.

"Suit up. Make sure you grab a mask. Even though the poor bugger has been removed, the stench will outlast religion" Creed quipped, flicking his cigarette out the window of the two-story brick rental.

Boston-Wright ripped the packet open and hastily pulled out the plastic one-piece suit. She didn't want to lag too far behind the team, nor did she want to hang around the scene too long either. The smell was horrific. No amount of training ever prepares you for your first corpse. They say the first one lasts with you forever and his burnt remains most definitely will. Welcome to the murder squad, Boston-Wright. You've got a doosey.

Boston-Wright stepped quickly but precisely throughout the scene to catch up to her team. Creed was speaking with Pratt, who gave Boston-Wright a welcoming rookie look, almost ignoring her as he kept conversing with Creed. Was it the fact that she was just a rookie or was she witnessing firsthand the silence of the boy's club? No matter what, Boston-Wright was going to show these old boys that she could cut the mustard.

"We're not a hundred percent sure, but we think our victim is Sam Thompson. The scientific team will let us know more later." Creed included Boston-Wright in the latest update. Boston-Wright heard him but didn't fully engage. His lips were moving, his voice blurred as Boston-Wright saw the actual death scene for the first time. Even though the body had been removed, the lingering smell almost took her breath. She wanted to vomit. Beads of sweat formed on her top lip. Her cheeks glistened with perspiration as she felt her body drain of blood. Quickly turning so as not to embarrass herself, Boston-Wright made her way to a window, the breeze cooling her skin and bringing her back to the present.

"It's okay, love. We've all experienced it. Would you like tea or coffee? I'll send Pratt to grab you one," Creed commented.

Shaking her head indicating she could carry on, Creed continued with his update. "We think the victim is male, about 21 years old. When we found him yesterday, his left wrist was handcuffed to the downpipe under the sink. He had been set alight, with an accelerant possibly being used to quicken the burn."

The sweats never really left Boston-Wright, her legs almost buckling as she visualized what might have occurred. Creed could see what was about to occur and quickly motioned for the troops to move back outside. Boston-Wright barely made it to the golden cane palm before it all came up. "See you back at the car," Creed shouted. Boston-Wright waved to indicate she heard him, but she was unable to speak.

Back at the station, Boston-Wright tried to keep pace with Creed and Pratt as they entered via the rear. The kitchen door almost took Boston-Wright out as Pratt let it go, failing to wait until she had passed through.

Boston-Wright took up a position at a vacant desk and grabbed a file, trying to make herself look busy. It was a coloured girl, stabbed to death about five years ago. The other files read with a common thread. All victims were coloured, black actually, and all were handcuffed when killed. The bodies had been found in Pottsville, Tweed South, Kingscliff, Hastings Point and now maybe Cabarita Beach.

Boston-Wright gave a sideways glance at Jack Creed while flipping through the case studies. He looked washed out. It looked as though he hadn't slept in months, his skin was dry from the lack of water and his five o'clock shadow looked like a week's growth. Boston-Wright kept thumbing through the file, trying to take the facts in.

"Pratt, I'm heading over to see Dr. Russell. Want to tag along?"

"Can I come too, sir?" Boston-Wright asked, feeling a bit like a first grader asking her teacher for permission.

"Sure, but you supply your own hanky this time."

Dr. Russell was expecting Creed. She had the charred remains on table three set in the corner and away from the main flow of traffic. The scientific team was used to seeing horrific sights, but even this one was a bit gut-wrenching for some.

Creed moved around the table, taking it in from different angles. It looked impressive, but Boston-Wright was unsure as to what it would achieve. He brushed past Dr. Russell, biding for the best position as the photographers moved around, flashing their cameras. Jane Russell carefully moved the blackened bones onto the side, hoping not to break any. The body's forearms were up close to his face, looking like he was trying to protect himself, but Dr. Russell assured the onlookers that was the result of muscles tightening during the fire. Her dry, somewhat quiet voice seemed to give her statement more authority.

"The left knee has taken quite a bashing going on the multiple fractures," Dr. Russell observed, "possibly broken with a mallet or sledge hammer. He was struck with considerable force.

"We found blood smears in the second bedroom, probably caused by dragging his body over the lino. Either he was trying to escape himself or the perpetrator dragged the body out of the room. No matter what, Jack, he suffered, most likely tortured over a period of time."

"So far the neighbours say they didn't hear a thing. No screams. Do you think he may have been drugged, Jane?"

Jane Russell gave Detective Creed a lingering stare. She was an old-fashioned girl for her 40 years, preferring formalities in her lab, especially in front of her staff. Titles should be used at every occasion, something her surgeon father instilled into her from an early age.

"The good doctor will enquire with toxicology to see if any traces can be found in the tissues."

Boston-Wright was trying to focus her mind on what was being said rather than looking at the body. She picked up on Dr. Russell's stance on casualness, repeating in her head a saying her Dad often said, "Casualness leads to casualties." That advice had kept Jo in pretty good stead, although it was no armor of protection when she met Brett Wright.

The sound of the electric saw finally got to Boston-Wright. Till then she was putting on a brave show, but the sound of metal and bone coming into contact had her running for the women's toilet. She just made it, slammed open the cubicle door and by the time she lifted the seat, she let fly with an almighty heave. Leaning over the bowl, glistening with perspiration, Boston-Wright braced herself then lifted herself back to a standing position. Feeling weak and somewhat dehydrated, she shuffled over to the basin, splashed some water into her face and sipped some water from her cupped hand. Looking into the mirror, Boston-Wright confirmed she looked like death warmed up. Now to face the boss, smart arse Pratt, and Dr. Russell's crew.

Creed met her in the hallway on the way to the gents. "Killed around 11pm Saturday night. Bloody amazing that nobody heard a thing," he said as he disappeared into the toilet. Creed was soon out and beckoned Boston-Wright to follow him out of the building toward the patrol car, doing up his zip as he walked.

"Did your old man snore?" Creed asked, turning to Boston-Wright.

"What? What do you mean?"

"Well if he did, he may have owned a nose clip. Snore–eze is one of the biggest sellers for that sort of thing. You could peg your nose until you become accustomed to this kind of stuff."

Boston-Wright nodded, gave a wry smile and slipped into the back of the patrol car. She thought Creed's knowledge of snoring preventative measures was a little too intimate for him not to be a user himself, but for now she'd keep those thoughts to herself.

Resting her head on the back seat, Boston-Wright closed her eyes as the patrol car sped back to the station, Pratt driving while Creed, one arm on the window sill, took in the scenery. The cool air helped Boston-Wright relax. Her thoughts turned to the victim. How did he end up in this situation?

****

Tossing his suit jacket at a chair as he passed by his desk, Creed moved to the incident room and entered the details he had learned from Dr. Russell and her team on a glass panel with a non-permanent marker. "I'm starving. I need food. Jenkins, grab me a ham, cheese and tomato toastie and a cappuccino from Jarrod's next door. Don't go down to Mary's canteen. Her coffee tastes like shit."

Constable Jenkins jumped up from his seat and quickly moved toward the back door. "Can I get you anything, miss?" he asked Boston-Wright.

It was nice to be asked but her stomach couldn't take food. "No thanks," she replied.

Pratt walked into the room as Creed continued to mark up the panel. The two men got chatting, completely leaving Boston-Wright out of the conversation. "Pratt, give O'Halloran an update and tell him we need a few more bods on the case. Let's reconvene at, say, 6 o'clock." Looking at his watch and thinking a little more, he continued, "No, that's beer o'clock. Let's make it 5."

"Sir, is there anything you want me to do?" Boston-Wright enquired.

"Check out the case files on the other murders."

Boston-Wright grabbed the files and moved over to the corner. Just as she rested her backside into the seat, Creed's booming voice could be heard all over the station. "I said a fucking cappuccino, Jenkins. What's this, a latte? Lattes are for fucking poofters." For all Jack's appreciation for fine clothing, his tongue could be rough.

Boston-Wright kept her eyes on the file. This was certainly a boy's club; something she would have to get used to if she were to survive in the murder squad it seemed. There was no offer for lunch. An instant coffee, International Roast to be precise, and an Arnott's biscuit would be her lunch today.

****

Four detectives and two constables entered the room, closely followed by Chief Superintendent

O'Halloran. It was 5 o'clock. Creed was in close pursuit, eyes gazing at the floor as he walked behind O'Halloran. Chief Super O'Halloran was everything Jack was not. It was clear why Creed loathed the man. Thinner, with a more athletic appearance, straight back and square shoulders, O'Halloran turned at the front of the room to address the troops, hands behind his back and a slight rocking on the balls of his feet. This copper did things by the book. So did Creed, but in a more relaxed way.

Giving the nod to Pratt, Creed called for attention. A hush came over the room as the officers listened in to the briefing.

"Our victim is Sam Thompson. Male, aged 21. We only have his mother's statement for now to go on, which is sketchy to say the least. On the night he was murdered she was in the mental health ward at Tweed Heads Hospital, self-admitted apparently. She's still away with the fairies, so we'll have to verify her statement when she comes back to Mother Earth." O'Halloran gave Creed a look of disapproval.

"Like the other victims, he is black and was handcuffed when found. But unlike the other victims, he is male. This might be our breakthrough, gentlemen. Uh, sorry, Smith, it's been a trying case.

Constable Carmel Smith smiled. We think of you as one of the boys. We need to move quickly on this one."

Boston-Wright was out of the loop having not been privy to all the info of the other cases. However, it seemed that Sam had walked home from Maccas after having a fight with his mate Harry Sturgess. Harry and the rest of the gang at Maccas never saw Sam alive again. Harry had phoned Sam several times that night but no reply. When his mother didn't answer the house phone the next day, Harry went over the Sam's house. Even though it was completely locked up, he could smell burnt timber and smoke. He called the police to investigate.

O'Halloran was not convinced that Sam Thompson was connected to the other killings, and he suggested it should be treated separately. Creed was seething. In his mind the cases all intertwined. He conceded that Sam was male but all had been tied before they were killed. "Sir, we need to stay on this. Thompson is our breakthrough," Creed said, looking at O'Halloran as if he would not take no.

"I'll run with it for now, Detective Creed," the Chief Super reluctantly quipped.

The team broke up and headed out the back door

as if somebody had shouted fire. It was beer o'clock, to turn a Jack Creed phrase. The junior constables were left to straighten the room and dispose of the empty Coke cans and dirty coffee cups.

Boston-Wright soaked up the atmosphere and reminisced about her late father. There must have been many times that the head of the table sat empty at dinner time over the years caused by incidents like tonight. She felt a sense of pride. She was living her purpose.

CHAPTER 2

The clock struck 1am. Jo was still at the station going over her files. She thought that by making her own notes she would get to know the cases better. She was right, but the process was long.

Jessica Campbell was the victim from Pottsville. Thirty-six, aboriginal, a prostitute and a drug user. To top it off, her old man constantly gave her a bashing just for good measure, he told the local police, who were often called to her Coronation Street flat by neighbours who heard her screams from the thumping Tony was giving her.

A pretty sad life. Left school at 15, in and out of jobs, then forced to perform services for the local male folk to make ends meet. She met Tony when she was 18 and he kindly introduced her to dope. By the time she was 20 she was a full-blown addict – ice, heroin, you name it. Tony was a lazy shit. He would force her into having sex with strangers, mainly tourists in the town.

When she would return home, he'd grab the cash and head to the pub, but not before giving her a belting for being 'unfaithful.'

Jessica's body was partly decomposed when police finally found her some four weeks after her death. Tony was naturally the number one suspect but was ruled out when it was determined that at the time of Jessica's death, Tony was in custody at the Pottsville Police Station having glassed a patron earlier that night.

Boston-Wright decided to call it quits. It had been a long day, her head was full, and she needed to sleep. The drive home was quiet. Her home looked uninviting. No lights on and a sense of eeriness filled the street. Now 2am, Jo had just a few hours before she would have to front up again.

****

Driving into the Kingscliff Police Station car park, Boston-Wright noticed it was full. Her only alternative was to risk the four-hour limit on the street. She hoped the local meter man would be kind to her brand-new Holden Cruze. It was the first time Boston-Wright had owned a new car. It was a bit of a celebration for saying good bye to Brett.

Glancing at the wall clock as it struck 9, Boston-Wright gave out an enthusiastic welcome to Carmel Smith as she entered the incident room. Trying to hide her lack of sleep, the welcome was a bit punchier than Boston-Wright would normally deliver, but she was hoping to get a favorable return from Smith and possibly bond with another female officer.

"Hi." It was spoken in a lackluster monotone voice with about as much enthusiasm as Smith could raise. Perhaps it had been the wear and tear of working in a station full of male policemen for 17 years that had sucked the life out of her, or maybe she was just feeling a little tired herself.

"Quiet day," Boston-Wright threw in, looking around the empty room.

"Nah. They're all in the briefing room. The meeting's been going for an hour," Smith replied while continuing to type on her desktop.

"Shit, why wasn't I told? Nobody said a word last night. Who's down there anyway?"

"The Chief Super, Creed, his goon mate Pratt and a couple of flat foots," Smith answered. "They are trying to convince the Chief Super that the Thompson case is linked and to get more resources.

If Creed can do that, we'll get more permanent officers on the case."

Boston-Wright stormed out and headed toward the briefing room. Arriving at the door, she noticed it was closed. Her heart missed a beat. Should she just barge in? What if Creed gave her a lecture about being late? She put her ear against the door but all she could hear was a muffled voice. Her listening was broken by the door opening from the men's toilet. Pratt came bouncing along, wiping his hands on his handkerchief.

"How's it going in there?" Boston-Wright enquired.

"Creed's struggling a bit with O'Halloran. He's got nothing new. The Chief Super isn't giving much away. We just need more bods permanently on the case and we'd crack it. But Creed and O'Halloran have history."

"Well let's hope he can pull a rabbit out of the hat." Boston-Wright thought better of entering the briefing room and decided to head back down the hall, leaving Pratt to rejoin the group.

Boston-Wright sat down at her desk and started reading about the third victim, Darlene Ferguson, aboriginal, 26 and a cleaner at the Hastings Point Caravan Park. Boston-Wright's mind flittered off momentarily to her family time spent at the

Hastings Point Caravan Park. It commanded breathtaking views across the beach to the ocean; one of the most serene holiday parks on the northern NSW coast. It was a favourite of her parents who booked each summer school holidays at the park until Jo left home to attend university.

But Darlene's brutal murder knocked the serenity right out of the park. Her strangled body, neck broken, was found wedged under the roots of a mangrove tree on the side of the caravan park 24 hours after she had went missing. She had been sexually assaulted and her naked body was covered in sand fly bites to add insult to her injuries. Once again, like all the other victims, she had been handcuffed.

Jack Creed, followed by Pratt, stormed into the incident room. He had a slight smile on his face, although Pratt displayed a nonchalant look that would win him a few poker hands. "Good news, team. The Chief Super is giving us more permanent back up. Smith, you'll be happy to know we are getting more admin support for you. Boston-Wright, you'll be with us for a tad longer."

Boston-Wright smiled cautiously, noticing Pratt's change of expression. Creed moved to the board and pinned Sam Thompson's photo to it, signaling the Chief Super had backed his scenario that all the cases were linked.

"Listen up, team. We've been given a small window to catch this bastard. Pratt, take a couple of lads and get back to Cabarita Beach. Have a look for any CCTV from McDonald's along the main drag back to Cypress Avenue. Ask at the Mobil petrol station if they have anything. We have a serial killer on our hands. Let's make Sam Thompson his last victim. On your way!"

Everyone else filed out of the room.

"Boston-Wright, you hang with me. I've got Sam's buddy, Harry Sturgess, coming back in for a chat." Boston-Wright was happy to be Creed's wingman. Looking like this might be another long day, Boston-Wright asked Creed if she could duck off to the canteen to grab some lunch. "No problems. Be back here at, say, 1pm."

****

"How was the slop today?" Creed asked as Boston-Wright returned, placing her bag beside her desk. Boston-Wright's look clearly expressed her thoughts. "Smith, grab me an egg and lettuce on multi grain and a cappuccino and bring it into Interview Room 2."

Creed and Boston-Wright made small talk before Smith returned about 20 minutes later. "Here's your sandwich, sir. There's a Harry Sturgess in reception with his father. I'll send them in, shall I?"

Creed nodded and moved around the other side of the table and sat next to Boston-Wright. In his mind, the thought of seeing two police officers when Harry walked in would hopefully give him a scare; not that he was a suspect, but no doubt he could provide some valuable information.

The room was eerily quiet. Even Boston-Wright felt nervous and she wasn't the one to be questioned. The arrival of Sturgess seemed to be taking forever. "Are you all right, Boston-Wright?"

"Yes, sir, but I just can't see how Sturgess would have anything to do with all those other murders. You did say they are connected, didn't you?"

"Yes, of course they are connected," Creed spat back while finishing up his sandwich and removing the crumbs with his right hand. "I know all the other victims are women, but the fact they are all aboriginal and were handcuffed when they were found is our connection. The handcuffs are not some kinky little toy you can buy in a sex shop; they are Smith and Wesson's. They are heavy duty."

Smith knocked and led Harry and his father into the interview room gesturing for them to sit opposite Creed and Boston-Wright. The starkness had Harry nervously looking around the room as he pulled his chair out to sit down. His father, on the other hand, was a little more hostile, demanding Creed explains why his son was being questioned in such a manner.

"Just routine, Mr. Sturgess. Your son was one of the last people to see Sam Thompson alive. We just want to fill in a couple of holes," Creed replied in a calm, if not monotone voice. Creed had already begun his little game. Speak softly, look confident and stay calm. Harry certainly appeared twitchy while his father was putting on his best daddy protection act. Creed understood that. He'd do the same if his daughter Melissa was in any strife, but his reactions would be less controlled.

"You and Sam were mates at school, right?"

"Yep, we met in Grade 8. Quite a while ago now."

"Sam have many friends? What about a girlfriend?" Creed asked, noticing Harry's eyes moving away to the corner of the room, away from his father.

"He had a few mates. We usually hung out together."

"And a girlfriend?" Creed pressed again.

Harry drummed his thumbs on the table, noticeable enough for Boston-Wright to give him a long stare and enough for his father to follow suit. "Yes, Kia was sort of his girlfriend."

Sensing there was more to Harry's response, Creed pressed harder. "Sort of girlfriend? Was there some tension there?" Harry shuffled in his seat, pushing himself back into the rest. Boston-Wright could see Harry was agitated.

"Was Kia the center of the argument you had with Sam that night? Is that why he stormed out of McDonald's and walked home?" Creed raised his voice. Harry's father looked anxious.

"He, umm, found out, uh, about me and Kia," Harry coughed up. "She wasn't his girlfriend anymore, well not really. I don't know why he freaked out so much." Harry's dad let out a huge huff of disapproval, wiping his right hand firmly across his mouth and chin.

"So what happened then?" Boston-Wright chimed in, thinking it was good for her to get in on the questioning. Jack Creed's facial expression told her otherwise.

"I paid the bill and ran outside. I saw Sam walking down the main drag, past the Blue Rose café. Then he crossed the road. It was pretty dark. I shouted out to him, but I guess he didn't hear me."

"Did you see him head down to Cypress Avenue?" Creed asked.

"Nah, that was the weird thing. He cut down Pandanus Parade. He must have turned at the Surf Club and walked along the nature strip." Creed knew the route well. The path cut in front of the Seaview Motel, Creed's home away from home. It was poorly lit at night. A few unused holiday homes between the motel and the surf club meant there was not a lot of light at night. The locals often took the path as a short cut to the Beach Hotel. It was considered safe, but not perhaps last weekend.

"And you didn't chase after him?"

"Nope. No point. I thought I'd call him next day after he had calmed down."

"Okay, Harry, that'll be all for now. Mr. Sturgess, you can take your son home. For now," Creed added, just to stir up the butterflies a little more in Harry's stomach.

****

Creed and Boston-Wright headed off to the lab to see what further findings Dr. Russell had come up with.

Jane Russell was methodical in her approach, painstakingly so at times. But this case wasn't throwing up any startling new evidence. She beckoned Creed and Boston-Wright to follow her over to a table against the wall where she had laid out photographs of all the victims.

"I think we already know all the similarities here, Detective. All female except for Sam. All aboriginal or black. All handcuffed. But this may interest you," she went on. "Look closely at the handcuffs," she said.

Reacting like a cat on a hot tin roof, Creed couldn't help himself by diving in with, "Yes, I know they are all Smith & Wesson's. Ridgy didge handcuffs," he replied with a smile like a Cheshire cat feeling proud of himself.

"Detective Boston-Wright?"

"Um," Boston-Wright said, stalling for more time to come up with something intelligent to say. "The lock on the cuffs is on the left wrist of all the victims," she said after studying the photos. She looked up at Dr. Russell, hoping she would not be shot down in flames.

"Exactly, Detective Boston-Wright! Chalk one up for the girls." Dr. Russell said. "We girls surely can pick up the finer details," she said smugly, giving

Creed a look of 'another one for girl power.' Creed just huffed and asked what the significance of that would be.

"Possibly, but not conclusively, the perpetrator is left-handed. Easier for him or her to lock with his or her left hand. One thing that is conclusive, though, is that the cases are all linked. There is one killer."

"Okay, great, let's get back to the station and fill in the newbies. They should have arrived by now." Creed beckoned for Boston-Wright to join him in the car. He walked swiftly and confidently with a sense of purpose in his step, his face showing an air of confidence that he was right from the start. The pleasure of showing O'Halloran he was a better copper was evident but contained.

The new troops had arrived, making themselves at home. Creed clapped his hands, drawing their attention and directing them to the incident room. Boston-Wright followed in quick step, keen to show her enthusiasm but feeling the pinch of only having an apple for lunch.

Creed quickly got through the formalities of introducing himself, Boston-Wright and Pratt to the new team. Amongst them some fresh- faced,' starry-eyed policemen and women who looked like they just stepped out of the Academy. The usual chain smoking, double chin, pot belly blokes exuding the look of, 'Yeah, yeah, we've been here before,' occupied the other chairs.

"Dr. Russell has confirmed Sam Thompson makes number 5. We need to get out on the streets and talk to everybody who was in the vicinity of McDonald's on Saturday night and may have seen Mr. Thompson walking home, especially after he rounded the surf club. At the moment we've ruled out Harry Sturgess, his mate, but we've told him not to go too far."

"Smith will have coffee and donuts for you all soon," Creed barked, trying to show his caring attitude toward his team members. Boston-Wright thought, "Great. A sugar fix. That's all I need."

"Ok, any updates while Boston-Wright and I were out? Over to you, Pratt."

Greg Pratt jumped up and stood beside Creed. "We interviewed Damian Walsh, a London lad, here on a working holiday. He's a 'dish pig' at the Bear Club, a gay bar next to the pub and across the street from Maccas. He was outside the club having a cigarette when he thinks he saw Sam leaving and heading down Tweed Coast Road."

"Any observations?" Creed asked. Boston-Wright quickly threw her hand up, wanting to show the newbies that she wasn't so new. All eyes were on her. She felt like she was at speech night back in Grade 8.

"We know Sam was wearing a white t-shirt with a black bear riding a bicycle on the front. Do you think the killer may have assumed Sam came from the Bear Club?"

Pratt chimed in to throw down his seniority by dispelling her theory with, "All the other victims were female," but Creed threw Boston-Wright a lifeline, complimented her initiative and asked one of the newbies to check on whether Sam may have had any gay tendencies. Boston-Wright appreciated the support.

"Let's call it a night and be back here bright and fresh in the morning," Creed ordered. The room emptied in seconds. The newbies climbed over each other to hit the carpark. Boston-Wright found her pride and joy all alone five minutes later.

With her stomach growling, she thought about a pizza as she drove by Dominos but decided bed was a better option.

CHAPTER 3

Boston-Wright was glad to be home, but the cupboard was bare. Perhaps she should have stopped for that pizza after all. Instead, a slice of multi grain toast and a rubbery piece of Kraft cheese on top washed down with black coffee, because there was no milk, would be dinner tonight. But grocery shopping was another task for tomorrow. Too tired to do any more case file reading, Jo set the alarm for 5am.

The alarm rang out and Boston-Wright hit the snooze button. These past few days were already taking their toll. She couldn't believe how whacked she felt and wondered how her older, overweight colleagues like Pratt kept up the pace. Creed, on the other hand, cut a fitter image for a fifty-plus man, and Boston-Wright guessed he just ran on adrenaline anyway.

It would be another hour before Boston-Wright

would surface, somewhat dazed as she stumbled from kitchen to bathroom eating toast and blow drying her hair. Looking in the mirror with toast hanging from the right side of her mouth, Boston-Wright momentarily stared at her reflection and wondered why she had man issues. But this was no time for self-analysis, another case file needed to be read before she headed off to the station. Besides, Brett was a two-timing arsehole anyway.

Victim four was Sharon Berg, an American Negress, holidaying in Australia. At 40-something, she had the body most 20-year-old girls would die for and their boyfriends would envy. Sharon was curvaceous and loved younger men. Like all the other victims, this cougar was also handcuffed. Then she was strangled with her bra and her panties rammed hard down her throat. Her body was found behind the Roxy Nightclub. She had left behind a twelve-year-old daughter in Tennessee. The poor girl was now a ward of the State. Boston-Wright placed the file on the coffee table, sat back into her couch, sipped her coffee and thought about Sharon's fateful holiday. Nobody should go on holiday thinking they might not return.

Boston-Wright's eye caught the clock. Shit. It was 7.45am and she would be late for the 8 am meeting. Quickly gathering her bag, she stuffed the file inside, grabbed her keys and rushed out the door, leaving the half-drunk cup of coffee on the bench alongside a plate of partly eaten toast.

Boston-Wright called Creed from the car. "Sir, I'm stuck in traffic. I'm going to be late," she said, trying to reduce the damage already caused, especially as it was only her third day.

"Meet me over at the lab, okay? And by the way, do you have the Berg file? Smith is going off her tits about the file missing."

There was deadly silence on the other end of the line. Boston-Wright realized she should have signed the file out. Looks like she had better buy a box of chocolates for Smith to smooth things over.

"I guessed so. Straighten it out with Smith when you get back. See you at Dr. Russell's soon."

Jane Russell met the detectives with her usual professional look, clipboard in hand, but today with a more perplexed gaze on her face. She called Creed and Boston-Wright over to the table and pointed out a fracture just below the left knee cap.

"Could this have happened on the night he was killed?" Boston-Wright asked.

"No," Dr. Russell promptly replied, "but I wanted you to see this. It's not the only broken bone in this poor lad's body. He's either been very clumsy or suffered a lot of abuse over his life."

Creed took a mental note of Dr. Russell's findings and asked Boston-Wright to check it out with the boy's mother. A strain clearly showed on his face. Creed was increasingly frustrated with the lack of new evidence in the case. With his head drooping, he half-heartedly waved goodbye to Dr. Russell and headed back to his Mustang parked in the carpark.

"Is this yours, sir?" Boston-Wright asked with a sense of amazement but also exhibiting an expression of childlike excitement as she admired the '67 fast back, navy in colour.

Creed momentarily got a spark back into his forlorn face. "Yes, this is my baby." His voice gushed with pride.

"Cool. Next time I'll leave mine behind."

****

Boston-Wright entered the incident room first while Creed stopped off to grab a coffee from the kitchen.

"Anything new?" Pratt asked, peering over the local newspaper, most likely studying the form guide.

"There were some extra broken bones on Sam's body. Maybe long-term child abuse? And you?"

"Watched a mountain of CCTV tape and interviewed our little gay dish pig Damian, although he insists he has a girlfriend. Probably bats both ways," Pratt mumbled while still fixating on the sports page of the Northern Star.

"Jim, what's the latest on the video tape?" Creed asked walking into the room.

"Damian has identified our boy Sam walking down Tweed Coast Road. The camera outside the Commonwealth Bank shows him walking by alone and then rounding the corner. The Surf Club camera shows him pushing through a few blokes outside the club, and then heading along the beach path to Cypress Avenue."

"And nobody followed him?" Creed asked.

"Nothing showing, boss."

Creed insisted the tape be rewound as all officers leaned forward, trying to pick up any little detail that may help them. Sipping coffee with his eyes firmly fixed on the television screen, Creed intently watched every millisecond of the tape while somewhat violating Boston-Wright's personal space. She felt a little uncomfortable, but now was not the time to give a woman's lib-type speech. She shuffled forward as much as she could, but Jack instinctively followed suit.

"There. The white Land Cruiser. It seems to be going slowly down the main drag," Boston-Wright chipped in. "Could the car be following Sam?"

Pratt didn't seem enthusiastic about Boston-Wright's observation. Perhaps without an identifiable number plate, it would be hard to narrow the owner down. Or perhaps it was just an anti-woman thing.

"Maybe it just looks like the Land Cruiser is going slow. Have a look at Sam in this frame. He's stopped, maybe a little dazed as to where he is. He doesn't seem to know where he's going. And then he turns down Pandanus Street. Why wouldn't he just keep going down Tweed Coast Road? Cypress Avenue runs off it," Creed observes, his index finger of his left hand tapping his top lip.

"Maybe somebody called out to him or he saw somebody he knew down toward the surf club?" Pratt threw in, adding to the endless list of possibilities. Nothing was getting the team closer to discovering the truth.

"Fast forward to when Sam pushes his way through a couple of lads outside the surf club,"

Creed says. "Here he goes. Blonde surfer type on the right with the beer in his hand. Look over his right shoulder, toward the beach. Who's the grey-haired dude almost in the shadows? He just seems to be a little out of place. Let's see if we can track down the guys outside the club and the older gentleman."

The team dispersed and Creed returned to his office, gently closing the door behind him. Running his right hand through his grey, short cut hair, he let out a sigh, grabbed a file and sat down. He was getting nowhere with the murder of Sam Thompson and he was clutching at straws trying to pull the other cases together. Aware the others may be looking in, he tried his best to make out he was just tired and that the case wasn't beating him, but nobody was 100% fooled. Waiting in the wings was O'Halloran, just urging him subliminally to fail.

Boston-Wright sensed his pain and gave herself a mental chat to step up. She grabbed a case file and started reading it again, hoping something would pop out.

"You're Bruno Boston's daughter?" Constable Smith asked.

"Yes, that's right."

"Great detective, your father. We all miss him. There was a big turnout for his funeral."

"Yes, I remember. Mum and I were thankful for that," Boston-Wright replied, appreciative of the comment but hoping Smith would change the subject.

"If your dad was running this case, we would have cracked it by now. I don't think Creed is up to it. And as for Pratt and the new boffins, not worth a pinch of shit."

"We'll get the killer, Smith. Creed will crack the case," Boston-Wright replied. With that, the moment of complimenting Creed was broken by his booming voice. "Boston-Wright, in here!"

Boston-Wright gathered her notebook, sprang up from her chair and quickly made her way into Creed's office, carefully closing the door behind her. By the tone of his voice she thought closing the door would be a wise move. Creed sat forward on this chair, tapping his pen on the desk, eyes down before addressing Jo.

"Not off to a brilliant start, are you, Boston-Wright?"

"How do you mean, sir?"

"Yesterday you threw up at the sight of our Mr.

Thompson on the lab table. Monday you were leaning up against a tree gasping for air after visiting the crime scene. And today, you were 45 minutes late. Not a brilliant start, wouldn't you say?" Boston-Wright's head dipped and dejection washed all over her.

"But in saying that, you are giving it a crack. Taking files home, reading up on the past cases. At least you are showing some enthusiasm, albeit you are a bit green. Dr. Russell thinks you're okay, praises all round. And of course, you are Bruno's daughter. Hopefully some of his genes have been transplanted in you. Let's be more conscious of the time, eh?"

Boston-Wright returned to her desk, a little bewildered. She was pleased her late nights and extra workload were noticed, but it seems not being sick over a dead body makes you a better copper. She sighed, sat down in her chair and tossed the notepad on the desk. She had hoped Creed was above the boy's club thing, but perhaps she was wrong.

Creed appeared from behind his desk and rallied the troops around. "Team, tomorrow we air on Channel 7, 9 and 10, including Prime and WIN Television. Expect an influx of calls from every lonely heart, drop kick to phone in. These fruit loops will test your patience, but it's all part of the process. And it'll be a long process. But we will catch this prick. Sam Thompson was his or her last murder. Grab some sleep and be back here at 8 o'clock sharp." He gave Boston-Wright a lingering stare.

****

Boston-Wright's cupboard still wasn't replenished, but at least she had milk. Her coffee this morning was more palatable as she tiptoed out into her courtyard wearing a fluffy dressing gown that hid her knickers and bra, and picked up the local newspaper off the dew-covered lawn.

"Pottsville Pyscho Killer Returns" the headline screamed from the Northern Star. Just what the force needed. Mass hysteria. She raced back inside, closed the door and quickly flicked on the Channel 7 Sunrise morning breakfast show. It was 7.05am and Chief Super O'Halloran was being interviewed by David Koch, the programme anchor. Great, Boston-Wright thought. Creed was going to be right. Every nutter in the world would be on the phone this morning. She sculled her coffee, got dressed and made her way to her car. There was no way that she was going to be late today.

She flung the back door of the Kingscliff Police Station open, nearly knocking over a couple of the new lads and proceeded with purpose down the corridor toward the incident room. The phones were already ringing off the desks.

Sixty-seven calls had come in the first hour. It was bedlam, but the families of the five victims needed answers. Time to suck it up and press on.

CHAPTER 4

The phones had rung hot, but the information was cold. Creed was right in saying that the lines would be jammed with every nutter south of the border. Boston-Wright felt like she had spoken to dozens of them all wanting to tell their life story but not really offering up any new evidence. The team was frustrated. Of the leads that came through, the newbies were assigned to start sorting through the information.

But on a more positive note, Harry Sturgess cracked in an interview with Pratt, confessing he and Sam did get into a physical altercation in the toilets at Maccas. Originally reluctant to say anything, Sturgess felt the heat from Pratt and was concerned about implicating himself any further in the death.

According to Sturgess, Sam challenged him about his relationship with his girlfriend. With that said,

Sam went to the toilet and Harry followed him in to sort it out. They got into a heated argument and Harry punched Sam hard in the stomach, causing him to buckle over. Without wanting to flame the situation, Sam picked up his tote bag off the floor and stormed out, leaving the restaurant. Harry gathered himself together and casually walked back into the restaurant and out onto the street to see if he could see Sam.

Pratt started flashing images of the CCTV through his mind. He didn't recall seeing Sam walking down Tweed Coast Road with a tote bag over his shoulder. "Are you sure Sam left with a bag?" he asked Sturgess.

"Absolutely. It's dark grey or black, made from canvas. It's Sam's major possession. He swept it off the floor, placed it und his arm and stormed out."

"What do you mean, major possession?"

"It was his dealing bag, man. The local cops knew Sam Thompson pretty well down here. He had been nabbed a few times in the past year. And that's why Melissa, his girlfriend, was dumping him. She was sick of him and his drug dealing. We all were."

"What was he dealing?"

"Mainly ice, sometimes E, whatever he could mix up."

Sturgess slumped in the interview chair. He felt remorseful as he replayed the argument with Sam in his head knowing that had they not fought, perhaps Sam may still be alive today. Pratt accepted Sturgess's description of events and decided to release him.

Pratt joined Creed and the team and brought them up to date with Sturgress's latest account of events. They would need to review the CCTV tapes again and conduct a search for the grey/black tote bag.

"From what I know about serial killers, they usually keep a token of their victim's possession, a keepsake to remind themselves of their deed. These sick bastards get pleasure from it, apparently. But I'd be surprised if our killer kept a tote bag."

"You're assuming the killer is a man and a bag would not be his thing," Boston-Wright asked.

"No. The bag would be too big. Too hard to conceal. They usually keep small tokens, like a lock of hair, jewelry and the like," Creed offered up.

"Maybe it's a drug deal gone wrong? Perhaps Sam owed somebody money."

Pratt rolled his eyes, dismissing Boston-Wright's lack of murder experience. Smith backed him up by fidgeting in her chair and turning away from Boston-Wright. Creed let out a small huff but was cautious not to stifle her enthusiasm and stem the flow of ideas in the future. God help them, they needed fresh ideas.

Over the next few days, the team sifted through all call messages. It was confirmed that Sam was wearing a tote bag on his right shoulder, which was mostly concealed from the cameras as he walked down Tweed Coast Road. They needed to find that bag. The killer's DNA could be on it.

Smith turned up an interesting call. She spoke to a lady, British accent, who believed she saw Sam talking through the window to the driver of an old Land Cruiser, close to the Bear Club. That would kind of fit into the CCTV tape that showed a Land Cruiser passing Sam slowly before he turned down Pandanus Street.

Creed ordered Smith to see if a number plate for the vehicle could be identified as he addressed the team. "Listen up. We need to go over all the murder victims' cases. Tom Langley, Jessica Campbell, Darlene Ferguson and Sharon Berg. Cross reference anything and everything!"

****

A fortnight passed and the team had come up empty-handed. The case was going nowhere. The Chief Super was up Creed's ribs demanding results. But nothing was popping. The case was heading south and if Creed didn't get a break soon, he'd lose his newbies and most likely the case to another team. Creed gritted his teeth at the thought of losing the case but more importantly allowing O'Halloran get one over him.

Creed pressed on with his grueling schedule. He was tired and the 10 cups of black coffee a day weren't helping. His diet was going to shit and the ciggies were making their way back into his routine. Black coffee and a packet of cigs a day was not a healthy option for a 50-year-old guy carrying a few extra kilos.

Yes, the lack of new evidence in the case was frustrating, but Creed's frustrations were amplified even further by the lack of not getting back to Brisbane to see his family. It had been weeks since he had visited his daughter Melissa in New Farm Clinic, causing him more angst. He missed his wife and daughter tremendously, but the case needed to be cracked.

The phone rang out on Smith's desk. The ring seemed louder than normal or maybe the team was desperate for some good news. Smith grabbed the call and identified the man on the other end as Peter Tebbit, a detective from Queensland wanting to speak with Creed.

Creed mimed to Smith for her to grab his details, suggesting he was out. Smith jotted down some notes which read that he had some knowledge on Creed's serial killer and wanted to pass it on.

"He's a fuckin' old has-been, bent copper from the drug squad in Brisbane," Creed responded thinking this was all he needed. "Give me his details. I'll call him later," he said reluctantly. Tebbit was one of the reasons why Creed had left the Queensland Police Force and transferred down to New South Wales. Not having a lot of time for the man, Creed was in no rush to call him.

****

Pratt and Boston-Wright hit the pavement from Maccas down Tweed Coast Road, stopping passersby and asking if they were in the area that fateful Saturday night. Nothing. Nobody seemed to be in the vicinity or just didn't want to be associated with being near a gay night club. In either case, this walking and talking to the public idea of Creed's was fruitless. Pratt expressed how pointless this random approach was and decided to return to the station.

Boston-Wright on the other hand decided to persevere. Jack Creed was an experienced detective and if he thought walking the streets and chatting to the locals could turn up a lead, then the least she could do was to give it a hundred percent. She entered the IGA Supermarket to grab a coke.

"$3 lovely," the cashier asked. Boston-Wright jerked her head up to eyeball the lady behind the counter. Not because the price was stiff, but because of her British accent.

"Are you the lady who spoke to Constable Smith a couple of weeks ago about the Sam Thompson case?" Boston-Wright asked.

"Not me, lovely. That'll be $3."

"No, it's definitely you. Smith mentioned your British accent and you called her 'lovely' on the call. I just want to chat," Boston-Wright insisted, although she couldn't believe her luck in just stumbling upon the woman while thinking that persistence does pay off.

"Hey, I'm busy. Are you going to pay for the drink?"

"Yes, I'll pay and then you can come with me back to the station where we can talk more formally."

"Listen, I don't want any trouble. I did my good

deed bit. Besides, I don't want Donny, the owner, to see me chatting to a copper. I've got a ciggy break in ten. I'll meet you around the side," the cashier said reluctantly.

****

Creed tapped the sticky note on his desk, eyeing the details of Peter Tebbit. The last thing he wanted to do was call a man he despised. He sighed and bounced the note on alternative corners, hoping the ink from the page would drop off and he wouldn't have to make that call.

Tebbit was everything Creed wasn't. A sleazy womanizer who thought he was God's gift to women. Flashy, loud, gregarious and seemed to have acquired assets way above a normal policeman's salary. Nobody else on the force drove a Mercedes, but Tebbit and some of his goons in the drug squad liked to flaunt their opulence. Creed realized the call had to be made, although he didn't hold a lot of hope in the quality of the information Tebbit could pass on. More importantly, Creed wondered what it would cost him. He was damned if he did or didn't. Boston-Wright burst in.

"You still here, sir?" She looked at the clock showing 8pm on the wall behind Creed.

"Where else would I rather be?" Creed sarcastically replied.

"I found the Pommy woman Smith spoke to, who identified the old Land Cruiser a couple of weeks ago." Boston-Wright exploded with enthusiasm while gasping for air as she tried to settle herself.

"Bingo!"

"And it gets better. She definitely saw Sam chatting to the driver. In fact, it was a pretty calm conversation, as if Sam knew the person."

"Any make on the number plate?"

"No, but she knows the family. They come into the supermarket where she works all the time." As Boston-Wright grabbed her notepad out of her jacket side pocket, she said, "His name is Mick Darlington, ex-Army but now retired. He lives across from the Thompson's with his wife, Kay."

"Well I guess that rules him out of being a member at the Bear Club," Creed threw in to a bewildered looking Boston-Wright. "Good work, Boston-Wright. Let's follow that up tomorrow."

Boston-Wright wrote up her notes and finally left the station around half nine, stopping by the Pizza Hut to grab a takeaway for dinner. Sitting in the drive through, a smile came across Boston-Wright's face. She knew she had made a breakthrough today. Her dad would have been pleased with her. The 'Bruno gene of persistence' was paying off.

****

Boston-Wright had a spring in her step the following morning as she entered the Kingscliff Station, greeted the desk sergeant with an enthusiastic 'good morning' and bounced into the incident room in readiness for the day's update. Creed gathered the team around. Boston-Wright looked nervously around the room with anticipation. Butterflies were going like the clappers in her stomach. She took a few deep breaths. Would she have to address the team?

"Okay, listen up. We've had a mini breakthrough," Creed announced, slightly more upbeat than usual. Boston-Wright fidgeted in her seat, straightening her back and giving the room her best little girl look.

"Dr. Russell has confirmed that the petrol used on Sam Thompson came from a BP petrol station. As we know, there is not a BP in Cabarita Beach. The nearest station is here in Kingscliff. Smith, get on to the owner and grab the CCTV tapes for the past two months. You know what, make it three."

56

Boston-Wright's head dropped and her shoulders stooped. She thought, no, hoped that Creed was going to announce to the team that she had made the breakthrough and finally get some recognition. She let out a silent puff of air.

"And Boston-Wright also found the UK woman who phoned in anonymously a couple of weeks ago and has identified the owner of the Land Cruiser. Good work, Boston-Wright."

Boston-Wright returned from the wasteland in her mind to the present with a bang. The smile on her face showed her appreciation to Creed for giving her some limelight. Pratt looked at Smith blankly, his left index finger going in a circular motion next to his left thigh but clearly out of sight of Creed and Boston-Wright.

Creed also announced to the team that he wanted Boston-Wright to go to Brisbane to interview Peter Tebbit. While it would have been a good option for himself to see his family, he couldn't stand to be in the same town as Tebbit, let alone the same room. A few of the old boys gave Boston-Wright the stare of 'teacher's pet' as they would have liked an all-expenses paid overnight stay at the 5-star Hilton. Boston-Wright smiled with contentment. Maybe she was moving ahead.

CHAPTER 5

It was still dark at 4.30am when Boston-Wright woke to get ready for her trip north to Brisbane. Queensland was an hour behind NSW time, making her early start feel even earlier. A quick piece of toast and vegemite washed down with a cup of instant coffee was all Boston-Wright could manage as she raced out the door to fire up her car for the two-hour journey to Police Headquarters in Roma Street Brisbane, home of Detective Sergeant Peter Tebbit.

The traffic flow through the Tweed was moving at a good pace, but a snarl at Elanora and Nerang slowed her down to a crawl. Boston-Wright anticipated this and had left early so as to make her 8am appointment. But the highway carpark at Springwood was another story, leaving Boston-Wright quite frustrated and somewhat anxious about being late. The road was a sea of cars barely moving, making Boston-Wright wonder why all these people would do this on a daily basis. Give her sleepy old Bangalow any day. Once through Springwood, the pace picked up and Boston-Wright was once again travelling at 100 klms/hour.

At 7.50am Qld time, Boston-Wright turned right off the South East Freeway onto the Turbot Street exit and then made her way along Roma Street to the Queensland Police Headquarters. The building was prominent, making a statement by taking up most of the block and just a short walk from the court precinct, where many criminals had met their day. Entering the customer carpark bang on five minutes to eight, Bob the attendant steered Boston-Wright toward a vacant lot and advised her that DS Peter Tebbit was on the 4th floor and to just take the lift.

Boston-Wright pressed the lift button for the 4th floor, tugging on her jacket with her other hand to straighten herself up. She brushed her fringe off her face, gave herself a bit of a shuffle to relax the nerves and focused on the ascending numbers. The doors opened and she made her way across the navy carpeted entrance with the police insignia woven into the fabric. Behind the bullet proof glass at the counter sat a fresh-faced constable who politely asked Boston-Wright to complete the security form while she fetched Tebbit.

A timber door flung open. There stood an overweight, 50-something year old man, combed back self-dyed hair and a beer belly hanging over his belt, flashing his pearly whites as if his good looks would melt any woman on the planet. Everything Creed had said about Tebbit was right before Boston-Wright in full color.

Holding the door open with his right arm, Tebbit beckoned Boston-Wright to enter his inner sanctum. "Where's that old grumpy prick Creed?" he bellowed, offering to shake Boston-Wright's hand. She reluctantly offered her hand, which was met by his, limp and sweating palm, while he directed her between his bulging stomach and the door arch into an open plan office area with private offices along the left perimeter. There was barely enough room, leaving Boston-Wright no option but to brush past DS Tebbit, something he knew would occur from previous invites. Sleazy. Just as Creed described as Boston-Wright made her way as quickly as she could inside, hopefully to be seen by other officers. At least then she would feel safe.

With his left arm pointing toward the third office along the wall, Boston-Wright made her way into Tebbit's private office. Thankfully, the wall to the open floor was made of glass. Boston-Wright felt a little uncomfortable in the presence of Tebbit.

Tebbit gave her the once over as he sat back into his desk chair, which squeaked as his overweight frame squeezed between the arm rests. Red-faced and the bottom buttons of his shirt gaping, Tebbit was not a pretty sight, let alone a healthy one.

"Where the fuck is Creed?" he barked at Boston-Wright. "I left a message that I had some info for his case and the prick doesn't have the decency to come up here and talk to me about it? Instead he sends the junior. What a bloody insult!"

"He was tied up, so he asked me to see you. I am on the murder case too," Boston-Wright replied, feeling somewhat inadequate as she applied pressure to her intertwined hands, trying to overcome her nerves.

"And that arsehole Pratt? He'd be out sipping lattes in some coffee shop, no doubt. Tied up my arse. Phone Creed and tell him to get off his butt and get up here. I will only pass on my info to the man leading the case. Not the help, sweetheart."

"Truly, sir, Detectives Creed and Pratt are tied up. Carmel Smith sends her best regards." Boston-Wright looked pensive, hoping she was making some in-roads. "You may know my father, Bruno Boston?" Boston-Wright hated hanging onto her father's coattails but sometimes he came in handy.

"You Bruno's daughter? Why didn't you say?"

Boston-Wright smiled as Tebbit recalled the good old days he had spent with her father. Nothing was new to her, though. She had heard the stories hundreds of times before. Maybe one day people will fondly tell stories of her, but for now she needed to get Tebbit back to the current day.

"So you have some information for us, Detective?" Boston-Wright butted in and tried to steer the conversation back to the case in hand.

"One of my informants may have whispered something in my ear. Is there a reward?"

Cheeky bugger, Boston-Wright thought. Creed had schooled her up prior to meeting Tebbit. Apparently, Tebbit had claimed a few rewards in the past under the guise of an informant, according to Creed. He was investigated about 5 years ago about some claim, but a lack of evidence didn't make it stick.

"No reward, detective," Boston-Wright put innocently but without confidence.

"No fucking reward. Five bloody deaths and no reward. You've got to be joking." Tebbit glared back at Boston-Wright, sizing her up to see if she was bluffing. "It's getting late, I've got another meeting and I'll need to chat to my informant to see if he wants me to pass his info on. Where are you staying tonight?"

Hell would have to freeze over before Boston-Wright imparted that knowledge to him. "Not sure. I may head back to the Coast," Boston-Wright delivered in an unconvincing tone, avoiding eye contact with Tebbit.

"Whatever, honey. Let's chat in the morning over breakfast. At the Hilton?" Tebbit smiled, knowing full well it was the Hilton where his interstate colleagues stayed when visiting Brisbane. Having shown Boston-Wright he was no dummy and not a man to be messed with, he quickly intervened with, "Nah, let's make it here at 9. Good morning, detective."

Boston-Wright stood, shook his wet fish hand, and left Tebbit's office. Riding the lift to the ground floor, she knew Tebbit had played her today and that Creed would not be impressed. She took some deep breaths as she exited the building and walked to the carpark. The clear blue sky and light breeze lifted her spirits and helped calm her nerves before she had to call Creed. At least a night in a 5-star Hilton luxury hotel would give her a boost. Pity she didn't have somebody to spend the night with her.

Hopping into her car, she returned to Earth at the thought of Peter Tebbit hitting on her.

Boston-Wright did a u-turn on Roma Street and headed toward Turbot Street, joining the traffic of eager drivers dying to get to their next appointments. She dialed Creed using the hands free.

"Not much luck, sir. I'm seeing him again in the morning. He says he's got some info but needs to clear it with his informant. You were right, he asked for a reward."

"Told you. Bloody bent copper. There is no informant." Creed let out a sigh of frustration. "You didn't tell him where you were staying, I hope?"

"I might be blond, sir, but I'm not stupid."

"Okay, Boston-Wright. Let's see if tomorrow brings some better news."

****

Creed rubbed his forehead with his thumb and index finger while gazing down at the paperwork on his desk. It had been four weeks since Thompson had been killed and the case was going colder by the minute. The Chief Super was looking for another update and he had nothing to give. He was losing his grip, and if the tide didn't turn soon, he'd lose the case to another officer. And that was not on Jack Creed's resume. He always solved his cases. He called Pratt into his office.

"Not more overtime, Jack," Pratt tentatively said. "The boys need a break."

"We are going nowhere, Greg. Dr. Russell phoned an hour ago. No DNA on Thompson. Fark! When are we going to get a break?" Creed let out his frustration. Smith looked up from her desk. She could hardly miss the outburst. Most probably the entire team heard it as well.

"And Boston-Wright? How did she get on with your mate Tebbit" Pratt asked.

"She's seeing him again tomorrow. Didn't get a lot out of the cunning prick today."

"Well, a nice steak and a bottle of red at Victoria's and a good sleep in a nice comfy bed should ease the pain. I'm sure Boston-Wright will be smiling. Did she have company?" Pratt said, looking down at Creed, who returned a distant stare. "Pray she didn't let Tebbit know where she was staying. He'd be there in a flash."

"Give her a break, Pratt. She's not that stupid or desperate."

****

65

Boston-Wright returned to the police headquarters at exactly 9am. Tebbit invited Boston-Wright into his office, again wedging himself between her and the doorframe. Boston-Wright gave him the look that spelt loser in volumes. He returned a sleazy smile, the booze evident from the night before as he burped with her passing.

Once again he squeezed into his office chair, his spare tyre hanging over his belt, giving full view to Boston-Wright of his hairy belly button. And to think this guy thought he had a chance with her the night before.

"So, what have you got, Detective Tebbit? Has your informant given you the okay?" Boston-Wright asked in a firm matter, wanting to wrap up this meeting as quickly as possible so she could return to Kingscliff.

"Um, he's not impressed, but here's what I got from him." Tebbitt realized it was futile to keep the mirage going on any further. "My mate is ex-Army. Served in Vietnam."

"Yeah," Boston-Wright nodded impatiently.

"Well, he read that all the victims had their hands tied behind their backs from the newspaper articles."

"Yes, but that's common knowledge, Detective. Like you said, it was in all the papers."

"But it's the way they were tied. With handcuffs."

Christ, this is like pulling teeth. Boston-Wright let out a sigh in frustration.

"They were Smith & Wessons, right? The same brand issued to the military police in the Australian armed services back in Vietnam. Your killer is a Vietnam vet. Bingo! Case closed," Tebbit let out with gusto, imagining himself as some sort of Sherlock Holmes.

Boston-Wright nodded cautiously, taking Tebbit's analysis in. "Thanks, Detective Tebbit. I must get back to the Coast."

"No lunch, honey?"

"No, Detective. A name has just popped into my head. Got to fly."

CHAPTER 6

Smith's mobile vibrated on her desk, causing a casual glance. It was Boston-Wright asking her to run a background check on Michael Darlington. It finished with a note to say she'll explain when she gets back to the station.

Smith, uncertain if she should proceed with such a request, immediately forwarded the text to Creed, who was sitting in his office drowning in a foul mood.

"What's this shit, Smith?" Creed barked after reading the sms. "Why the bloody hell didn't Boston-Wright text me directly? I am the commanding officer on this case. Jesus Christ! Give me strength."

Smith thought she had better stick up for her fellow female officer and decided to run the background check, hoping it would turn up something to help Boston-Wright and perhaps get her out of a pasting from Creed. But no such luck. Darlington was a clean skin, not even a parking fine in the last ten years.

The traffic heading down the M1 was at a snarl. The usual bottleneck at Springwood was particularly heavy today thanks to an overturned semi spilling its entire load across three lanes, slowing traffic to just one. The rubberneckers sent the traffic down to 10 kilometers an hour.

Boston-Wright decided to use her time more wisely and exited the highway, taking the service road and looking out for a café to grab a snack, having not eaten breakfast at the Hilton. She was now starving and desperately needed some fast food to beat her lightheadedness. She drove past the usual names of McDonalds, Hungry Jacks and Subway until she spotted Harry's Highway Diner, wedged between a Toyota dealership and a used car lot.

Boston-Wright pulled into the kerb and walked inside, glancing back up to the highway, which was still in gridlock. The establishment was full of car salesmen feasting on hamburgers and fried chicken; it looked like feeding time at the zoo. Boston-Wright chose a burger from the Bain Marie and ordered a cappuccino to go. There was no way she was dining in.

The coffee tasted like boiled milk, something like Grandma would have served up. Boston-Wright opened the car door and tipped most of it into the gutter. The burger wasn't much better. She was wondering on which day the burger was actually placed into the warmer; it couldn't have been today. Maccas would have been a better choice but she was hungry. She polished it off in quick time, giving herself heartburn and leaving tomato sauce stains on her trousers.

But it was only twenty minutes down the M1 from Springwood when Boston-Wright realized the contents of her burger were not fresh, needing to dart into the Mobil service station to the inner sanctum of the lady's toilet. Boston-Wright was furious not only about Harry's fine food, but the fact she had passed up a 5 star breakfast at the Hilton just so she could fit in with that sleaze bag, Tebbit. Now she was paying for it. Two more stops later, she finally arrived at the Kingscliff Police Station a little after 1pm.

Smith was waving her hands furiously at Boston-Wright, trying to get her attention before Creed spotted her. "The old boy has blown a fuse about you texting me earlier. Wondered why you didn't go to him direct." Boston-Wright listened on with a perplexed look on her face, sneaking an occasional glance toward Creed's office. "And by the way, there's nothing on Darlington. Not even a parking ticket," Smith finished as Creed interrupted in a booming voice for Boston-Wright to enter his office.

"Boston-Wright, who is running this case?"

"You are, sir," squeaked Boston-Wright.

"Then why the fuck are you texting Smith with info about the case and not me?"

"I just needed Smith to run a background check so I would have all the facts before I discussed my meeting with Tebbit, sir."

"Well, we have procedures here, Boston-Wright. It may not look like it at times, but it's simply called communicating with the team, especially the boss. So, let's have it. Who is Michael Darlington?"

Boston-Wright raised her left hand to her forehead, wiping away a bit of perspiration before she spoke. It had been about thirty minutes since she last visited the lady's restroom at the BP Chinderah, but she wasn't totally out of the woods. Her stomach continued to flip flop and she was ready to exit Creed's office at any given moment.

"Michael Darlington lives near Thompson. I've looked at Pratt's interview with him and there's not a lot there. Smith didn't turn up anything either."

She glanced at her notes while sporadically looking up at Creed, whose face was showing signs of disinterest.

"But there is one thing. Tebbit said the handcuffs used on all the victims were made by Smith & Wesson."

"So?" Creed chimed in with a distinct lack of enthusiasm.

"Those handcuffs are extremely rare. You won't find them around here. In fact, the biggest buyer of Smith & Wesson handcuffs is the military police and according to the purchasing officer at Canungra Barracks, they no longer buy this brand of handcuffs. They use zip ties instead."

"Go on." Creed rustled in his chair now with a bit more interest in what Boston-Wright was saying.

"In fact, the Army hasn't bought Smith & Wesson cuffs in over a decade. According to Sergeant Duffy, if we had a pair, they would probably date back to the eighties, maybe even the seventies. Now this is what sparked my interest, sir. Tebbit said we should be looking for somebody who served in the Vietnam War."

"Bloody Tebbit and his theories," Creed dismissed.

"Not so fast, sir. Michael Darlington is a Vietnam

Vet and has spent most of his working life since the war working in security."

"And so you think he's the type of guy who may use handcuffs in his job?" Creed said in a skeptical if not dismissive tone, most likely fueled by the fact that Tebbit had sewn a seed in Boston-Wright's mind and she was listening.

"It's the best lead we've got to go with so far, sir."

Trying to give his newest team member some credence, Creed decided to run with Boston-Wright's line of thinking even though he thought he'd be humoring the idea at best. Looking back at her while trying to muster some enthusiasm, Creed asked where Mr. Darlington now resided.

"Across the street from the Thompson's."

"Great." Creed's enthusiasm increased until Boston-Wright interrupted.

"But he's not there now. According to the neighbour, both he and his wife have been away for about a month," Boston-Wright replied. "Keen caravanning enthusiasts, I believe."

Greg Pratt burst into the incident room.

"Just got off the phone from the manager at the Big 4 Caravan Park in Yamba. That guy Darlington was there about a month ago."

"Bingo. Around the same time or just after Sam Thompson was murdered," Creed said with a look of renewed confidence on his face with Boston-Wright looking back, hoping for some form of recognition, perhaps a little slap on the back. Nothing. Jack Creed wasn't the back-slapping kind of guy.

"Call the manger bloke, O'Neill, and tell him we'll be down to see him tomorrow. Yamba is about three hours from here. We'll go in the Mustang. I'll put the sunroof back. Better bring a scarf or something so your hair doesn't get all messed up," Creed commented with a smirk on his face while glancing at Pratt.

"Maybe I could borrow some of your Brylcreem, Pratt?" Boston-Wright fired back to wipe the smile off his face. Creed gave an acknowledging nod to Boston-Wright – she could mix it with the boys.

****

Boston-Wright slipped into passenger seat of the '67 Mustang. It was a little lower than her car and certainly lacked the mod cons. No airbags. No coffee cup holders. It was certainly all Jack Creed, though. Cutting through the back streets of Kingscliff, Creed roared the v8 muscle toward the Pacific Highway at Chinderah.

74

Creed seemed to be in his own little world. A '70s rock station belted out Led Zepplin and the Stones with Creed keeping rhythm on the steering wheel. There was little conversation. Boston-Wright, sporting a New York Yankees cap, sat back and enjoyed the view. The silence was a little uncomfortable but welcoming at the same time. It was the first time she and Creed had been in such close proximity since she started in the Murder Squad. The trip gave her time to assess the man and think.

The entrance to the Big 4 Van Park was impressive. A row of well-manicured hedges defined the driveway as Creed parked in the guest spot next to the reception office. Sitting behind the counter, Tony O'Neill greeted the detectives by name as they entered. Perhaps Creed's sports jacket and Boston-Wright's business suit gave them away, as other guests would arrive in board shorts and sandals.

O'Neill had blended into the resort lifestyle. The former Gold Coast real estate agent had traded his shirt and tie for t-shirts and boardies ten years ago, grew his hair longer and slipped into the Yamba lifestyle with ease. A mad keen surfer, O'Neill had found his utopia.

"We wanted to talk to you about the Darlington's. I believe they have been staying in your Park?" Creed opened the questioning.

"Yeah, Mick and Kay. Nice old couple. Got a Jayco 26. Smart unit. Yes, they have been here, but they moved on earlier this morning," O'Neill replied. "Everything all right with them?"

"Yes, we're just making some routine enquiries," Creed said, trying to keep the tone lighthearted and the conversation flowing. As an old copper, he'd learnt a trick or two about getting people to talk freely. Make them feel comfortable and they just might drop a little tidbit that could blow a case wide open.

"Did they say where they were heading?" Boston-Wright piggybacked off Creed.

"No, they didn't, come to think of it. In fact, they left a bit unexpectedly. They were booked in for another day," O'Neill commented while glancing at his booking sheet. Sure, there was a fancy computer on the desk, but it seemed that O'Neill was a bit old school. Creed nodded while subconsciously acknowledging that both he and O'Neill were of a similar vintage, both a bit computer illiterate it seemed. O'Neill, on the other hand, certainly appeared more relaxed than Creed, though. Heavy tanning certainly aided a few extra wrinkles, and in some way Creed was secretly envious. Boston-Wright broke his daydreaming with another question.

"Really? That's interesting. Do the Darlington's come here often?"

"Yes, they've been here quite a few times," O'Neill replied, thumbing his way back through the booking sheet but coming up empty. Swinging his chair around, he rolled over to a book shelf and grabbed another booking book.

"Here we go. They were in about six months ago," he said, pointing to an entry.

Creed looked at Boston-Wright. The time was around the same time Sharon Berg was killed.

"Any chance you could go through the other booking sheets, say over the past 12 to 18 months, and let me know what other dates the Darlington's stayed with you? Here's my card. You can email me your findings to this address here," Creed pointed out as he gave his card to O'Neill.

Creed thanked O'Neill for his time and ushered Boston-Wright back to the car. "Let's grab a coffee before we head back. I know a little place on Coldstream Street." Jack thundered out of the Big 4

Caravan Park, down the street, finally coming to rest outside the Caperberry Café.

Creed gave Boston-Wright $20 and asked her order him a flat white and anything that looked good in the cake cabinet while he took up a pew at an outdoor table and started to look though the messages on his iPhone. Boston-Wright returned and passed over the change. Creed was sitting back in his chair, tie loosened, sleeves rolled up and legs crossed. This was one of the first times that Boston-Wright had spent with Creed out of the office. He seemed more relaxed, more normal. Boston-Wright liked Creed when he was more 'George Clooney' than 'Mr. Grump.'

Creed sat on his seat, stony faced. He was churning through a back log of unanswered calls. A dress shop next to the café caught Boston-Wright's eye but the window dressing told her the price tag would be way out of her police detective's wages.

"What do you think, sir? Could Darlington be our man?"

Creed shrugged his shoulders. "A bit early yet. But you never know."

Not the sort of response Boston-Wright had been hoping for. It was the best lead they'd had in months and the best Creed could do was to shrug his shoulders. Boston-Wright felt a little dejected.

"Oh, by the way, good work today. You tagged along nicely with your questions, Boston-Wright."

Jo felt a little better and tried to keep the conversation flowing. Pregnant pauses of silence were uncomfortable and she still had a three-hour drive back to Kingscliff.

"How old is your daughter, Creed?"

"Melissa, she's 19. Lives with her Mum in Brisbane when she's not in the clinic."

"Clinic?"

"It's not something I talk about, Boston-Wright. Melissa copped a fair bit of bullying at school, which led to an eating disorder, depression, that kind of thing. There are better facilities in Brisbane; that's why they stay there."

Boston-Wright's face reeked of shock, but she put on her best 'okay, that's normal' look. "So, you're not divorced then?"

"Nope, happily married for 20 years. And you? Got a boyfriend, or what do they say now, a partner?"

"Nobody special. Since Brett and I got divorced, I've been a little man shy," she replied with a smile.

"But you've kept his name or were you hoping for

a quick update?" Creed commented, hoping to get Boston-Wright to bite. But she didn't, although the squeezing of her hands was probably a fair indication that she was not overly pleased with Creed's comment.

"The name Boston would certainly get you into the right circles in the force," Creed remarked with eyebrows raised.

"I don't want an easy ride because of my father, sir. I'll do it my way. Perhaps we should head back."

The 10-kilometer trip back to the highway was quiet. Creed seemed to be a million miles away, probably mulling over the case while Boston-Wright had thoughts about her dad and wondered if she would ever be out of his shadow. Neither spoke. Creed idled up the ramp before giving the Mustang a full throttle for the three-hour drive back to the station. It would be dark before their work day ended.

The carpark at the station was poorly lit. Creed escorted Boston-Wright to her car, suggesting an early night so they could start a fresh in the morning. It was kind of an old-fashioned thing to do, escort a girl to a car, but Creed was old fashioned. He still opened the car door for his wife. Boston-Wright liked the feeling of protection. It was something she always felt with her father. He would often say that his job was to protect the two most important girls on the planet and both she and her mum always felt safe in Bruno Boston's care.

Jo decided on an early night. A piece of cheese and two whole meal crackers would be dinner tonight. Thoughts of her dad speaking to her flashed through her mind, sometimes interrupted by the voice of Jack Creed. There were similarities in their mannerisms, perhaps that's why she liked being on Creed's team.

****

Boston-Wright arrived to Creed already addressing the team in the incident room. A little embarrassed but somewhat annoyed, she took her seat. Nobody told her of a team meeting. Still the fifth person on a four man team, she thought.

"We've identified a Mick Darlington as a person of interest. Ex-military police and security. Likes to travel. We are checking on his latest movements now. He was last seen at the Big 4 Caravan Park Yamba, a place he's visited before around the time Sharon Berg was murdered," Creed described.

"According to the manager at the park, Darlington was a bit of a handyman and would do odd jobs for people while he travelled. Helped the cash flow, apparently," Creed continued. "Let's call around other caravan parks within, say, three hours' drive of Yamba to see if a Mr. & Mrs. Darlington are in residence. Maybe the manager bloke O'Neill will dig something up in the meantime."

Smith called Boston-Wright to one side. "It may be worth a call to Dad's Army. It's an organization that employs retired men to do odd jobs around the place. Just a thought."

"Dam good one, Smith. I appreciate the heads up." Jo smiled to a beaming Constable Smith, a sign of the girls sticking together.

An hour later Ted Dillinger, an organizer with Dad's Army, phoned Boston-Wright back to say that a Michael Darlington of Cabarita Beach was on their books. In fact, he was currently doing some work, fixing a rear deck, for a Mrs. Weatherly in Casino about 40 minutes west of Yamba.

Bingo! Boston-Wright put down the phone and rushed into Creed's office, quickly closing the door behind her.

"I've found him, sir. Mick Darlington is in Casino."

CHAPTER 7

Creed gathered the troops for a quick update. There seemed to be an air of confidence filling the room. Creed seemed taller. His white French cuffed shirt looked crisper; his Armani black sports jacket recently dry-cleaned. Boston-Wright observed that he was cleanly shaven and a dash of Bulgari Aqua wafted her way. With shoulders back, Creed began.

"We've found Michael Darlington. He's doing some work with Dad's Army in Casino. Boston-Wright and I are going to head down there now." Pratt looked at Smith and rolled his eyes. He was starting to feel left out, not like a copper who had 27 years' experience. He gave Boston-Wright a glare.

"Mr. Darlington is just a suspect, nothing more, so I don't want you telling anybody. It does not leave this room. The last thing we need is for the media to hear about it and send a posse down to Casino and whip the town up into frenzy. Got it?" Creed stared down each member as they acknowledged his wishes.

Creed placed Darlington's file on the center table and suggested the team have a read of it. There wasn't much to go on, but he wanted to make sure everybody was up to speed with the man's history.

The phone rang in Creed's office as he motioned toward his desk, inviting Boston-Wright to follow him and close the door. Creed snatched the phone off the receiver and placed it to his ear.

"Yes, Chief Super. Boston-Wright and I are heading down to Casino now. We want to have a crack at our man before he clams up and starts shouting for a solicitor." Creed sighed and rolled his eyes as the Chief Super told him the obvious, that they needed to do this by the book. No slip ups.

"I need to fix up a couple of things here, Boston-Wright. Get yourself ready. If you need morning tea, grab it now. We leave in 15 minutes."

"Your car or mine?" Boston-Wright said, tongue in cheek. Creed responded appropriately by waving her out of his office.

The two-hour trip to Casino was more talkative than their journey to Yamba. Perhaps Boston-

Wright was feeling a little more at ease with Creed and vice versa. The two discussed the case, interview tactics and the time slipped by. At exactly 1.50 pm, Creed's Mustang was pulling into the driveway of the Glen Villa Resort Park.

The manager was a short and portly man, receding hair and flush red cheeks. Obviously, a keen beer lover, Tom Dooley also loved a smoke. He wheezed over the booking sheet, adjusting his glasses as he squinted to find the Darlington's park site.

"Straight down the end, the last on the right. Site #44. Mrs. Darlington just drove out but I think Mick is still there. He wasn't in the Land Cruiser," the manager remarked.

Creed knocked on the metal door of the Jayco and took a step back. After a few minutes a croaky voice replied.

"Yes?"

"Mr. Darlington?"

"Yes," he said, even more cautious now. "Who is it?"

"The police." Pause. "May we come in?"

The door hatch was unlocked and Creed and Boston-Wright entered the van. It was quite spacious with a bedroom at one end and all the mod cons throughout including a microwave, flat screen television and an ice maker fridge.

To the left, sitting in the lounge area was Mick Darlington, a small framed man around 70 kilos, grey thinning hair with a matching beard, the upper moustache stained by tobacco. On the table was a packet of Drum and Mick was carefully placing some tobacco into a Tally-Ho paper and skillfully rolling a cigarette with one hand. Darlington appeared calm.

"Is this about the noise complaint, officer?"

"No, it's more serious than that," Creed replied pulling out his badge. "I'm Detective Sergeant Jack Creed and this is Detective Constable Jo Boston-Wright." Darlington scanned both badges of the officers and gave them due respect.

"Can I offer you tea or coffee? Let me just check if we've got milk. My wife's just gone to the supermarket." Darlington said opening the fridge door.

"No, we're fine, thanks, Mr. Darlington. We want to chat to you about a murder we are investigating," Creed replied, trying to gain control of the conversation.

"Murder? Anybody I know, Detective?"

"We would like you to accompany us to the Casino Police Station to continue this conversation. Are you willing to do that?" Creed asked.

"Well, I'm starting to think this is a bit weird. You come in here, asking me to accompany you to a police station, but you won't tell me who we are discussing. I think I have a right to know, Detective Creed" Darlington commented with eyebrows raised.

"Mr. Darlington, we need you to come with us to answer some questions about a murder case we are investigating. We can arrange legal representation for you there."

"No need, Detective. I'm happy to answer your questions. I don't want to appear to be unhelpful. Let me call a solicitor friend of mine. He can meet us there. Better to be safe than sorry, eh?"

"Pete, it's Mick Darlington here." Silence. "I'm in the van with a couple of detectives who want me to accompany them down to the police station. Some murder or something. They think I can help with their enquiries. Any chance you can pop into the Casino station? Thanks, mate. See you then." As Darlington clicked the stop button on his mobile phone, he shuffled toward the bedroom to grab his shoes. "He can meet us there in about an hour."

Outside, Boston-Wright wished she had talked Creed into bringing her car or at least a standard issue police car. Folding the seat forward, Boston-Wright climbed into the back of the Mustang, perching herself in the middle of the seat. Darlington got into the passenger, pulled on the seatbelt and glanced around the car.

"I'm guessing this is not standard issue or is New South Wales police on a budget? Nice ride though," he said as he nudged himself into the leather seat. Darlington was ever so cool. Ice cool, in fact, perhaps a little unnerving to the detectives.

Darlington telephoned his wife to let her know he was on his way to the police station to help them with their enquiries. By the way the conversation was going, it was obvious that Mrs. Darlington was a little concerned, but Mick Darlington just allayed her fears with, "Everything is all right, love. I'm just helping them out," and then continued talking. He finished the conversation off by letting his wife know he'd be home for dinner, which he had in the slower cooker on the bench. Nothing fazed Mick Darlington.

Creed drove to the rear of the station to avoid any possible attention at the front, quickly escorting Mr. Darlington through the rear door, down the hallway, past the kitchen to an interview room specially set up for him and Detective Boston-Wright. The Casino Police Station was a far cry from their usual Kingscliff station. It was a much older building, a little worn in parts but loaded with colonial charm. The sandstone walls could tell a pretty story or two.

Mick Darlington was shown in to interview room 2, a small room, no windows and a wooden table with public service issue four chairs. Boston-Wright directed Darlington to take a seat with his back to the wall while she sat opposite, closest to the door. The room felt damp, had a musky smell and was poorly lit. But none of that seemed to worry Darlington. He just sat patiently in his chair, occasionally giving Boston-Wright a smile.

Creed slipped out to the carpark to have a smoke and hoped to catch Darlington's solicitor upon arrival. A 911 with personalized plates 'LAWYER' slipped in beside Creed's mustang. Peter, as it turned out, was Peter Carter, one of the northern river's best solicitors, the go-to lawyer you called when you had to get off. Proficient in the technicalities of the law, Carter had gotten more drunk drivers off charges than any other solicitor in the area, much to the annoyance of the local constabulary.

Creed knew he would have to be on his A game.

"What's this all about, Detective? Seems highly irregular," Carter expressed clutching an old battered brown leather briefcase.

"I want to talk to your client about the murder of his neighbor Sam Thompson and another four murders over the past the past 10 years," Creed explained.

"What? Mick Darlington, a murderer? Are you crazy? Carter stopped in his tracks, looking like a stunned mullet.

"No. We think there is a fair bit that links all these crimes together."

"So, I take it my client is not under arrest," Carter enquired at the bottom of the rear steps into the station.

"No, just doing everything by the book," Creed assured as he held the rear door open and escorted Carter toward the interview room.

The clicking of the door handle broke the silence of the room as Carter entered, shaking Darlington's hand and giving him a look of assurance. Creed sat next to Boston-Wright, pulling his chair in close to the table and reorganizing some files on the desk. He leaned across Boston-Wright and turned on the tape recorder, announcing the start of the official interview.

"Present is Mr. Michael Darlington; Mr. Peter Carter, solicitor acting for Mr. Darlington; Detective Jo Boston-Wright; and myself, Detective Jack Creed. The time is 3.20pm. Mr. Darlington is not under arrest and has come here voluntarily to assist us with our enquiries," Creed stated for the record.

"Wait a minute. I wouldn't say voluntarily. More like a bit of heavy coercion," Darlington jumped in. This was the first time the detectives had seen their guest lose some of his coolness. Creed gave Boston-Wright a side glance.

"Can you confirm that you served in Vietnam," Creed asked

"A fat lot of thanks we got for it," Darlington bitterly remarked.

"I'll take that as a yes. I believe you were in the Military Police?"

"Yes, that's right." Carter made some notes but the answers didn't surprise him. He already knew this about his client.

"And after the war you worked in the security industry?"

"Yes, that's also true," Darlington replied, fidgeting in his seat.

"Where are you going with all of this, Detective? My client hasn't got all day," Carter chipped in, needing to say something to justify his $250/hour fee.

"So, I'm assuming you would have used handcuffs when you arrested people," Creed enquired.

"If they needed restraining."

Creed decided to switch direction, wanting to leave his last question lingering in the mind of his suspect, hoping it would play some mental tricks on his cool demeanor. He opened the folder on the desk and took out a photograph of Jessica Campbell, a prostitute from Pottsville, showing it to Darlington while explaining verbally for the tape what he was handing over.

"Ever see this woman?" Creed asked.

Darlington grabbed the photo, carefully stared at it, and politely said no as he tossed it back toward Creed.

Creed pulled out the photos of the other victims, each time announcing their name for the record and each time Darlington denied knowing any of them.

"Can you recall where you were on the 17th of January this year?" Creed asked.

"Detective, I'm not sure. Working somewhere, perhaps."

"According to your employer, Dad's Army, you were in Hastings Point repairing a fence for a Mr. Daniels."

"Well, if you know where I was, why the bloody hell are you asking?" Darlington said, raising his voice. Carter tapped him on his thigh, indicating to remain calm. Creed knew he was getting to Mr. Darlington and gave Boston-Wright another sideways glance. He then passed over the photo of Darlene Ferguson, a cleaner at the Hastings Point Caravan Park who was handcuffed, then strangled to death and her body discarded in nearby scrub land like a dirty rag.

"This lady, Darlene Ferguson, was murdered on January 17. She worked at the Hastings Point Caravan Park, the same place you stayed at, Mr. Darlington." Creed raised his voice and gave him a stare of death.

"Come on, Detective, that's a bit presumptuous," Carter intervened. Creed knew it was a bit thin, but it was worth a try.

"You'll notice all the victims were handcuffed, Mr. Darlington. Did you ever bring any souvenirs home from the army or your security job by way of handcuffs?" Creed asked calmly.

"This is ridiculous. I'm a happily married man. None of that kinky stuff goes on in my house. Now, since I'm not under arrest, I want to leave," Darlington remarked, his calm exterior slightly penetrated.

Boston-Wright escorted Darlington and his solicitor out of the station. She returned to the interview room and gathered the files into her bag. Creed was slouched back in the chair, tie loosened and looking rather glum.

"How do you think that went, sir?"

"How do you fucking think, Boston-Wright? Up the shit! That bastard was as cool as a cucumber. He gave us nothing. He seemed to know our every move. Our Mr. Darlington has been interviewed before and I'd say often in spite of him 'never been issued a parking ticket'. Let's get out of this shit hole. We've got a two-hour drive ahead of us." Boston-Wright gathered her things, avoiding eye contact and made her way to the car. This was going to be one of those quiet drives back to Kingscliff.

****

The team milled around the incident room, waiting for Creed and Boston-Wright to return. As the pair walked in, an air of expectation filled the faces of everyone waiting for them.

"Nothing concrete, team. We tried to rattle his cage but Mr. Darlington is very cool. Too cool, in fact. I think he knows the interview system well. Let's call it quits for tonight. Who's up for a beer? My shout." Creed said as he grabbed his jacket off the back of his seat and headed out the door. Pratt followed in pursuit and a couple of the new boys tagged along.

"How did it go, Jo?" Smith asked.

"Like Creed said, fairly ordinary. I think Mr. Darlington played us in one way, and then in another I felt sorry for him."

"Sounds like he played to your emotions, Boston-Wright. How would you feel if that were your father being interrogated today?"

"Creed did all the talking. I just kind of sat there."

"So, you might as well not have been there then," Smith remarked.

Boston-Wright gave a half smile, picked up her bag and headed out the door. No point going to the pub with the boys either. Truth be told, she probably wasn't even missed.

Dinner was another toasted cheese sandwich and a cup of tea. Smith's comment had hit a nerve. She was not being noticed. After all these months, she still didn't feel part of the team. Picking up a photo of her father, she commented, "Dad, why can't I be like you?" She placed the photo back on the sideboard, turned off the lights and went to bed. Tomorrow is another day.

CHAPTER 8

With Darlington free, the case was once again dying a slow death. The recently expanded team seemed to be a waste of resources and the Chief Super's hatchet men decided to reduce the numbers by two.

Creed had received a call from Dad's Army verifying Darlington's whereabouts around the time of the Berg murder. There was nothing concrete that could tie him to any of the other murders except that Thompson was a neighbour, which did not make him guilty of any crime.

Creed handed the files of the other victims to a new team member, hoping a fresh set of eyes may just dig something up. Boston-Wright got the Darlene Ferguson file, the cleaner at the Hastings Point Caravan Park. Darlene's mother took her own life not long after her daughter's murder, unable to cope with the loss. There was a phone number for

Darlene's aunt, who still resided in the area. Boston-Wright decided to give Joan Watson a call and meet up for a chat.

Boston-Wright pulled up outside Joan Watson's cottage in a quiet col-de-sac three streets from the beach and the Hastings Point Caravan Park. The house was a quaint cottage, a small verandah at the entrance protected by a bull nose corrugated iron roof. The property could have done with a fresh coat of paint, but the gerberas and hibiscus trees gave the exterior a cheery feel.

Joan Watson was expecting Detective Boston-Wright. She stood up from her rocking chair and gave her a warm welcome, steering her toward the couch next to her rocker. A pot of tea and a plate of Arnott's biscuits sat in the middle of the coffee table. On a side table next to Joan's chair was a photo frame proudly showing off a younger Darlene Ferguson.

"She was a very pretty girl, Mrs. Watson," Boston-Wright commented.

"Yes, she did a little bit of modelling after she left school. We, my sister Alice, Darlene's mother, I mean, had high hopes for her then. She could have gone to Sydney and made it big," Joan went on.

"But she never got the break?" Boston-Wright

asked curiously while biting into a Scotch Finger biscuit.

"No. She met Daryl Jones, a no hoper dropout, and her life spiraled downhill. Alice and I tried to talk some sense into her, but hey, when you're 18 and beautiful, you know everything. The only trip Darlene got to go to Sydney for was to attend the abortion clinic."

Boston-Wright empathized with Darlene's aunt, who continued to pour more tea. Joan pulled out a photo album and proudly went through each picture offering up a little story on a few. Darlene was a bright girl but seemed to get into the wrong company. After the Daryl fiasco, Darlene moved into a flat with a couple of school chums in Hastings Point. Her mother preferred she stay at home, but she wanted her own freedom. She got a job in a local boutique and everything seemed to settle down.

"Then she up and vanished. Met some bloke, much older than her, and moved to the Tweed," Joan elaborated.

"Then she came waltzing back into town with new clothes, jewelry and was throwing money around like water," Joan commented, flicking her head back as she said it. "But her mother and I thought she was on the game. You don't get that sort of money just being a secretary, if you know what I mean."

"And did anybody question her about this or try to stop her?"

"Several times, Detective, but she just left. We didn't hear from Darlene for four years. Her mother was heartbroken."

"But she did finally come back, right?" Boston-Wright asked.

"Oh yes. When she needed us. Skin and bones. She looked like death warmed up. Apparently, the old boyfriend had her on the game and was pumping her full of heroin. She left us as a beauty queen and returned as a junkie."

"That must have been heartbreaking," Boston-Wright replied.

"It took us years to get her cleaned up. It was my husband Dennis who got Darlene the job at the caravan park. And look what happened there." Joan placed her hand over her mouth as she shed a few tears. Boston-Wright couldn't work out if she had felt responsible or that she was just upset for her niece, but in either case Boston-Wright felt her grief. She patted Joan's hand and excused herself.

Boston-Wright sat at the junction. The Pacific Ocean rolled into a pristine sandy beach. Turn left and she would head back to Kingscliff, about a twenty-minute drive. But instead she decided on an off chance to turn right and head into the Pottsville police station to see if anybody remembered Darlene Ferguson.

Duty Sergeant Brian Lavers greeted Boston-Wright as she entered the station. His well-worn, wrinkled face immediately told her that he had been around. Maybe he could help her.

"I'm Detective Constable Jo Boston-Wright and I'm doing some work on a murder case. Have you got anybody here who may have known Darlene Ferguson or worked on her case?" Boston-Wright asked.

"I did, love," Lavers replied. "How can I help you?"

"How long did you know her?"

"I knew the family. She was a real looker when she left school. I know her mum had high hopes for her. Then that bastard Langley got his claws into her. Prostitution and drugs, totally ruined her life," Lavers explained.

"Langley? Do you mean Tom Langley?" Boston-Wright asked.

"Yes, that's him. Scumbag!"

Boston-Wright paused for a moment. For the first time there seemed to be a connection with the other murder victims. Langley and Ferguson knew each other, but the connection was never made until now. With Langley being killed further up the coast, it was probably reasonable as to why nobody had put two and two together. A case of one police station not talking to another.

Boston-Wright thanked Lavers and dialed Creed from the car but her call went straight to his message bank. She left a message saying she had found a connection between Ferguson and Langley and would discuss it with him in the morning. Being nearly 6pm, Boston-Wright decided to exit at Cabarita Beach and head home for an early dinner.

Unmotivated to cook, Jo stopped at Wok On Thai. Jason, the owner, saw her pull up and immediately started preparing a chicken Penang curry and steamed rice, Boston-Wright's staple order. As she entered the restaurant, she noticed a tall man, nicely dressed, with his back to her leaning on the counter eying the menu. There was a sense of familiarity, and when Boston-Wright was within a meter, he turned.

"Simon," Boston-Wright said in a startled voice.

"What are you doing here?" She tidied her hair and straightened her suit jacket.

"Down for the weekend," Simon replied with a surprised tone, his eyes lighting up at the sight of Boston-Wright.

Boston-Wright recognized his interest and thoughts of their brief relationship happily flooded back into her mind. Simon was the first man she dated after she and Brett separated. It was a hot and steamy romance with many a wild night spent at The Seaview Motel in Cabarita Beach but it was over as quick as it began. Boston-Wright never found out why except that Simon stopped calling.

"You're looking great, Jo. Have you been working out?" Simon asked.

"No, just healthy eating and a busy work schedule," Boston-Wright replied, lying about her eating habits but appreciative that Simon noticed her figure. Her hopes of a dinner invite tonight were rising.

"So are you dining in or grabbing a takeaway?" she asked, ready to change her dining plans at the drop of a hat.

"No, I'm getting a takeaway. Miranda is waiting back at the motel. We are getting married on Saturday," Peter said sheepishly.

"Oh, wow! Congratulations, Simon. I'm, um, very happy for you both. Hope it all goes well."

Jason appeared, as if on cue, delivered Boston-Wright's curry and she exited the restaurant. The drive home was filled with cursing comments in her head. How could she be so stupid to think an old flame would want to ask her out after not speaking for over ten months? How desperate was her thinking that she could pick up where everything had left off and perhaps tonight she might have gotten lucky? As she pulled up in the driveway at home, Boston-Wright leapt out of her car, slamming the driver's door with an almighty thud of frustration. She was so wound up. She tossed her curry across the kitchen bench where it would sit for the rest of the night.

****

The team gathered in the incident room and went over each other's findings for the past 48 hours. Pratt had tracked down the sister of Sharon Berg and spent the afternoon interviewing her. She moved from the US at the time of Sharon's murder and now resided in Bangalow, on a small farm, living a bit of an alternative lifestyle.

Pratt found it difficult to relate to her organic

passion and didn't get a lot of information about Sharon. He relayed there were a lot of uncomfortable pregnant pauses throughout the afternoon and he was glad to be out of the place. Her home had a distinctive odor and Pratt was confident that if the drug squad were to raid the premises, some cannabis would most likely be found. But he was not about to pinch a 50 year old hippy over a couple of grams of hooch. One thing was determined, though. Neither she nor Sharon had ever heard of Mick Darlington.

Smith was up next. She revisited Tom Langley's file, trying to look for similarities between all the other victims, but Langley was so far removed. The fact that he was male didn't match up with the other female victims. The only thing she could immediately link him to the women was the colour of his skin. There was a photograph of Langley and a group of people, perhaps friends, at the Tweed Heads Hotel but she was unable to identify any of them.

Boston-Wright leaned forward and inspected the picture. She smiled and placed the photo back on the table, eagerly waiting her turn to talk to the group.

"And, Boston-Wright, what do you have for us?" Creed asked.

Boston-Wright described the pain Darlene Ferguson's aunt still has today over Darlene's murder. "She went into great detail, almost blaming herself for the way Darlene had gone off the rails," Boston-Wright told the group. "Both she and her sister tried everything to get her away from an older boyfriend, who they never knew the name of, let alone met. It was just tragic."

Boston-Wright went onto explain that after she left Ferguson's aunt, she headed to the Pottsville Police Station where she caught up with Sergeant Brian Lavers, who was most helpful.

"He confirmed that the older boyfriend of Darlene Ferguson," she pointed to Smith's photograph, "was Tom Langley," said Boston-Wright, thumping the photograph with her index finger on the table.

"Bingo! We have a connection!" Creed let out with excitement.

Pratt, not wanting Boston-Wright to be glorified with this finding, piped up, "How was this missed earlier? Surely the aunt must have known?"

"Apparently not. Lavers did mention it to Darlene's mother, but as we know, she took her own life soon after. I suppose she had forgotten to pass it onto her sister," Boston-Wright remarked, giving Pratt a cool look.

"Still doesn't mean the murders are linked, though," Pratt commented, desperate to get the upper hand. Boston-Wright was aware of his little game and decided not to prolong the discussion. She walked back to her desk, thoughts of old dinosaurs flashing in her head. Creed called out to her from his office.

"Good work today, Boston-Wright, especially the little trip to Pottsville Station. Lavers is as honest as the day is long. Now I've got another lead to follow up. I'll pick you up at 7.30."

"Ok, sir, I'll see you in the morning," Boston-Wright replied, gathering her notebook and turning to leave Creed's office.

"No, I mean tonight. See you in an hour."

CHAPTER 9

Boston-Wright arrived home in a flurry. Throwing her bag onto the lounge, she made her way to the kitchen and opened the fridge to assess her dinner options. They were limited, again. A loaf of bread, some Kraft cheese slices, a shriveled up tomato and wilted lettuce. With the sandwich toaster warming up, Boston-Wright quickly scampered into the bathroom to lightly freshen up. A quick wash of her face and some fresh lipstick would be all that time allowed.

Right at 7.30 her doorbell rang. Tucking her blouse in with one hand, the other holding a half-eaten toasted cheese sandwich, Boston-Wright opened the door to a freshened Creed, sporting a new shirt and a waft of cologne. Boston-Wright was a little surprised at how well he had cleaned up and in such quick time.

"You eaten, sir?" Boston-Wright asked, gathering

her jacket and bag as she closed the door behind her and trying to keep up with Creed.

"Yes, I grabbed a quick bite," Creed replied, not looking at Boston-Wright as he adjusted his seatbelt and started the engine. Creed liked to keep his private life private and he could sense Boston-Wright was fishing for answers he preferred not to give. He decided the cold shoulder treatment might be sufficient hint for her to stop in her tracks. It worked.

"So where are we off to, sir?"

"I've arranged for us to see Charlie Warburton of Dad's Army in Tweed Heads. He runs the Northern Rivers branch."

****

A little after 8pm, Creed was pulling up outside the warehouse of Dad's Army in the Tweed Industrial Estate. The concrete building looked relatively new and was a mix of office and storage facilities. Creed pressed the door security, announcing himself and Boston-Wright, and was immediately let in. Unlatching the door, the team made their way up the carpeted staircase to a mezzanine floor office area. Warburton greeted the detectives at the top of the stairs and escorted them into the boardroom.

The polished timber table was surrounded by twelve high-back leather chairs. A buffet cabinet and a small bar fridge were against the back wall. The gyprock walls were a shrine to happy customers who used Dad's Army services and included a framed map of Australia, highlighting their Australian offices.

"Can I get you a tea, coffee or water?" Warburton offered.

"Water would be great," Boston-Wright replied, trying to be sociable while receiving a burning glare from Creed.

"And nothing for you, Detective Creed?"

Jack shook his head.

"Perhaps a wise move. Audrey has just gone home and I'm not the best tea or coffee maker." Warburton commented with a chuckle.

He invited the detectives to take a seat and asked how he could help. He expressed his concern that one of his trade people might be involved in a serious crime.

"This is just routine, Mr. Warburton. We need your help to hopefully eliminate Mr. Darlington from our enquiries," Creed outlined.

"It sounds serious, Detective, especially as you've both come up here tonight. Does he know you are here?" Warburton asked.

"No and there's no need for him to know either," Creed replied, giving a worried looking Warburton a firm stare.

"But what has he done? Nothing to do with kids, I hope," Warburton said with a surprised look on his face.

"No, no nothing like that. Have you got me his job schedule over the past year like I asked for?"

"I really would like to know if our organization is at risk, Detective. We have a good community name and we can't afford it getting damaged. We deal a lot with old people and you can imagine the reaction if our name was attached to some scandal," Warburton stated, still fishing for details of the crime.

"He's helping us with a murder inquiry," Creed let out with a tone of frustration. "The schedule please," he continued, his arm outstretched.

Warburton fumbled some papers and produced a hand written sheet of dates. "Christ, he hasn't killed somebody, has he?"

"He's just helping us. And thank you for your help." Creed and Boston-Wright stood and bid

Warburton good night. "We'll keep this to ourselves," Creed said as he and Boston-Wright descended the stairs and left the building.

"Fancy a drink, Boston-Wright?" Creed asked as he joined the M1 and headed back to Cabarita Beach.

"To be honest, sir, I'd prefer an early night."

****

Creed gave Boston-Wright a backhanded wave as he thundered out onto her street, probably to the annoyance of her neighbours, who were just woken up by the sounds of a growling V8. Boston-Wright headed for the shower. She was looking forward to washing the day away but she also realized she had let an opportunity slip to further stamp her place on the murder squad. A drink with Creed would have been good. Surely, he wouldn't have marked her down for not attending. The warm cascading water felt good but thoughts of self-doubt still niggled away. Tomorrow would be another day to impress.

Boston-Wright lay back on the bed and let the day slip away. It was a lonely life being a copper. There was a lot of strain on a relationship, as she had already experienced. Perhaps Creed had the right blend; work away from your spouse and catch up periodically. He seemed to have a good marriage; Boston-Wright assumed.

****

The next morning the team gathered in the incident room and carefully went over the work schedule of Mick Darlington supplied by Dad's Army. The report showed Darlington was painting a house in Pottsville during the same time Jessica Campbell was tortured then murdered. Darlington also did some cabinet work near the Roxy nightclub when Sharon Berg was killed. The buzz in the room was growing.

"Looks good enough for me. Let's arrest Darlington," Creed exclaimed.

The team looked excited, but Pratt suggested Creed run it by the Chief Super first. The evidence they had was highly circumstantial and they needed to dot their 'I's and cross their 'T's before they rushed into anything. Creed took a deep breath and nodded.

The Chief Super was even more cautious. He acknowledged to Creed that they were making progress but his information was circumstantial. It had to be more than a coincidence to make this stick. Get it wrong and the press would have a field day. The simple fact that Darlington was in town when a murder occurred did not make him a guilty man. O'Halloran vetoed any arrest until Creed could come up with more concrete evidence.

Creed returned to the team clearly frustrated. A look of despair covered their faces. They had been working so hard to crack this case and it seemed everybody was working against them, including their own Chief Super. But they also realized everything had to be perfect in order to make the case stick. O'Halloran did give them one glimmer of hope, though. They needed to search Darlington's house.

Creed recalled that Darlington would be back from his Casino work this morning, so he organized the search warrant and the raid to occur this afternoon. Two marked police cars carrying four constables from the Kingscliff Station, an unmarked Ford sedan with Pratt and Smith inside, and Creed and Boston-Wright in the Mustang arrived at the corner of Tweed Coast Road and Cypress Avenue at precisely 3.30pm. Creed quickly spoke to the team on the footpath, explaining the importance of being thorough. They were watched by peering eyes from the upstairs dental practice.

Creed's Mustang roared into the driveway of Mick Darlington's house, backed up by the other officers. Darlington, who was washing his caravan on the side of the house, looked up, stunned. He quickly looked at other houses on the street and caught glimpses of venetian blinds clanging as neighbours looked through.

"You've certainly made an entrance, Detective," Darlington said in an annoyed voice as he glanced up to his stunned wife at the top of the stairs and a Jack Creed striding toward him waving a piece of paper.

"This is a search warrant for your property, including your car and caravan, Mr. Darlington," Creed confidently explained as he directed the constables past Mrs. Darlington and upstairs into the house.

"What's going on, Michael?" a frightened Kay Darlington let out as her eyes welled with tears.

"Nothing, my love. The detectives just want to look around. Show them the house and make sure they don't break anything. Otherwise we'll sue," Darlington calmly told his wife while giving Creed an intent look.

Boston-Wright raced up the stairs to calm Mrs. Darlington and suggested that Carmel Smith sit with her in the living room. The home was a modest three bedroom, highset. The floral-patterned sofa had seen better days but the protectors on the armrests had probably added a few more years. In one corner was a Jason recliner rocker, blue leather, facing a medium sized television. The windows were covered with a combination of drapes and venetian blinds, something Smith had turned down to give the Darlington's some privacy from nosy neighbours. Mrs. Darlington appeared to be quite upset but Smith did her best to keep her calm.

Boston-Wright moved down the hallway to the first door on the right, the master bedroom. The floorboards squeaked as she walked, slightly softened by the imitation Persian rug that covered them. The bedroom was gloomy. The blinds were drawn and the room appeared stuffy, perhaps because of the lack of fresh air while the couple had been in Casino. A tallboy dresser in dark timber stood against the far wall. The dark colour made the room look drab, not helped by the peeling, light cream walls. Boston-Wright thought it ironic that a man who does handy work for others could not spend some time doing odd jobs on his own house.

Boston-Wright went through the hanging clothes in the cupboard, placing her hand inside the pockets of Mick Darlington's jackets and trousers. He was obviously a modest dresser with only two pairs of long trousers and a jacket, all of which exhibited labels known to Best & Less. There again, the man came from a non-privileged life, so Jo wasn't expecting Hugo Boss.

The other half of the dresser housed Mrs. Darlington's clothes. Again, a coat and a couple of blouses hung neatly from hangers. The chest of drawers contained nightdresses, underwear and the like. The bedside tables had loving photos of the couple, one from their wedding day and the other from a holiday by the beach somewhere.

Boston-Wright moved past the bathroom where two of the constables where going through the cabinet, fumbling their way through the toothpaste, brushes and razors. She stopped long enough to notice the pristine condition of the bath tub and basin and secretly wished hers looked that clean.

The next room was set up as a bedroom with a slightly more masculine feel. Camping and woodwork magazines adorned the bedside table and a small laptop computer on a desk sat in one corner. The left-hand side of the dresser had more of Mick's work clothes in it – checked shirts, King Gee shorts and a pair of Blundstone work boots, similar to what her dad had owned. The other side of the dresser was more like a storage area for files and paperwork.

Boston-Wright returned to the living room while allowing the other officers to continue searching the bedrooms and the rest of the house both up and downstairs. Creed had allowed Mick Darlington to join his wife; it seemed to have comforted her.

"Was it necessary to go to Charlie Warburton, Detectives?" Mr. Darlington asked.

"Just collating information, Mr. Darlington," Creed replied, pacing the floor, hoping for a constable to rush in with some incriminating evidence.

"But you told him you were investigating a string of murders. Was that really necessary? It's just that it's difficult to get work at my age and we need it to supplement the pension. This kind of stuff doesn't help."

"We are trying to be discreet, Mr. Darlington," Boston-Wright piped in.

"Yeah, sure you are. King Kong here roaring up the driveway, four cop cars with badges blasted all over the place parked outside my house. Very discreet, Detective," Darlington replied. Boston-Wright looked at him with some sympathy while

Creed continued to look through the house.

"I haven't murdered anybody, Detective," Darlington expressed to Boston-Wright while holding his wife's hand, gently stoking it to add some comfort to a distressing situation.

"You see that photo on the wall?" He pointed to a black and white picture of their wedding day. "It was the happiest day of my life. I married my childhood sweetheart. I would never jeopardize what we have," Mick Darlington explained to Boston-Wright with tears in his eyes. Boston-Wright bit her bottom lip as thoughts of her own parents' close relationship flashed into her mind. She looked at Mrs. Darlington and gave her a nod of assurance.

Creed walked around the room, giving Boston-Wright a glare as he walked by her. He could see the old couple were having an effect on Boston-Wright, something he didn't approve of. He needed a clear thinking, levelheaded police officer on the job, not one whose emotions were pulled up and down like a yo-yo every time some doddering old man gave a rendition of his wedding vows.

"I need to take some items with me, Mr. Darlington, and I need you to sign for them. I also want you to check that we haven't damaged anything," Creed explained to a wide-eyed Mick Darlington as he directed the Darlington's around their house.

"I'll see you in the car, Detective Boston-Wright," Creed commented as he walked off.

****

The other police officers drove away from the property, Pratt and Smith transported the confiscated goods. Creed calmly reversed out the driveway, then placed the Mustang in drive as he idled up the street before rounding the roundabout and heading back to Kingscliff.

"What the fuck were you doing in there, Boston-Wright? Playing how to win friends or something?" Creed let out in a fury.

"No. I was just listening to Mr. Darlington's story and observing how he interacted with his wife." Boston-Wright shuddered as she moved closer to her door, wishing now that she had taken her own car.

"And what did you observe, Dr. Phil? Is Mick Darlington our murderer?" Creed asked in a patronizing tone.

"No, I don't think he is. He couldn't bear to be separated from his wife, sir."

Creed looked Boston-Wright in her eyes. He could see her intensity and to some degree had to agree with her. There wasn't much revealed in today's search.

CHAPTER 10

Pratt and Smith were huddled in the corner when Boston-Wright arrived the following morning.

"Creed not in?" she asked, getting a shrug of the shoulders from Smith and a mumble from Pratt.

The team looked pretty dejected. Nothing was falling into place. The incident room door swung open and the Chief Super walked in with two goons following close behind heading straight for Creed's office. Boston-Wright immediately dialed Creed on his mobile.

"Where's Detective Sergeant Creed? On the afternoon shift?" O'Halloran barked.

Boston-Wright began to speak as Creed burst through the door and marched toward his office, looking a little worse for wear. Boston-Wright recognized he was still wearing yesterday's clobber. She dropped her head and got on with her work as one of O'Halloran's minders closed Creed's office door.

"Here comes the chop," Pratt whispered to Boston-Wright and Smith. "The bean counters would have been in O'Halloran's ear by now."

"It's only been a couple of months since the death of Sam Thompson. Surely they'll give us more time than that?" Boston-Wright queried.

"It's all the other cases as well, Boston-Wright. It's becoming too costly to have all of us on board for this," Pratt commented, trying to show his years of experience in such matters.

A few hours ticked over. Smith delivered a platter of sandwiches and a fresh pot of coffee into Creed's office around noon. The mood was somber. Creed looked like he had been dragged over the coals.

"Months and months have gone by, tens of thousands of dollars have been spent and we have nothing, Creed," O'Halloran remarked, staring down his target.

"We are exhausting every single lead, Chief Super."

"You place me in a very difficult situation. I need to scale this back or bring in an entirely new team and that means more expense."

"Then let me and the team keep going. We still have a few loose leads we are working through," Creed responded with a somewhat desperate look on his face.

"Sam Thompson doesn't even match the other murders, Creed. Single black male as opposed women, except for Darlene Ferguson's boyfriend, I suppose. If you can't connect Darlington to these crimes, can you eliminate him?" O'Halloran asked.

"Possibly, sir," Creed replied in an unconvincing tone.

"I need more than possibilities, Creed. I've got the Assistant Commissioner up my ribs. There are budget cuts coming and he wants a big bang for his buck. Unfortunately, today you haven't given me too much hope."

"Give me another month, sir. With the same team."

"Creed, you've got a week."

O'Halloran and his henchmen left Creed's office, their eyes focused on the exit and not giving a glance to the rest of the team. There was definitely segregation between the ground floor and the first floor staff. It felt like the Gestapo had just left the building.

Creed called Smith in and asked her to check on

flights to Sydney. Darlington had spent a fair bit of time there, especially around the period of the Kings Cross murders where a number of all black prostitutes were savagely killed. Coincidently, these murders all involved the victims having their hands tied behind their backs with handcuffs and occurring in between the Tweed Coast murders. It was a long shot and required more funding but Creed had a hunch. One thing he did know for certain is that psychopathic serial killers never get enough killing to satisfy their hunger. The Thompson murder would not be the last unless the perpetrator could be caught.

Creed called Boston-Wright into his office. As she passed Pratt's desk, she heard, "Who's the teacher's pet now?" but decided not to give it a millisecond of response. That was Pratts' issue, not hers. She was just doing her job.

"We're off to Sydney in the morning. Smith is finalizing the bookings now. Meet me at Coolangatta Airport at 10 for an 11 o'clock flight. We could be there for three days."

Boston-Wright left Creed's office, exhibiting a beaming smile overplayed especially for Pratt as she strode past. Gathering her bag, she bid the team good night and headed home, excited about her three days away in the big smoke, even though there would be little time for relaxation.

****

Creed was already onto his second cup of coffee and Danish as Boston-Wright entered the Qantas Club Lounge at Coolangatta Airport. It was her first time in a member's only lounge and she felt an air of importance as she flashed her entry card to the receptionist on her way in. The lounge was busy with a mix of businesspeople and holiday makers as Boston-Wright made her way past the buffet, through the maze of tables and tub chairs to Creed, who had positioned himself in a prime window setting with commanding views over the tarmac.

"Good morning, Boston-Wright. Help yourself to the buffet. We're boarding in half an hour. Tony, the barista, makes a great cappuccino. Think you could grab me another?" Creed returned to the Financial Review, barely giving Boston-Wright a moment to put down her bag and settle. A roll of her eyes was completely wasted on Creed, who was now immersed in the latest corporate happenings on page three.

Boston-Wright walked over to the buffet. She couldn't believe the selection of fresh fruit, yoghurt,

126

cereals and Danish pastries. The fresh strawberry yoghurt and a croissant looked tempting as she put them onto a plate and made her way to Tony to place her coffee orders.

She had barely sat down when the attendant made the first boarding call for their flight to Sydney. Boston-Wright quickly spooned up some yoghurt while cursing Creed under her breath for making her hurry her breakfast. Creed was oblivious to her angst and just kept on reading his paper, in no rush to join the boarding queue.

Ten minutes later they were both relaxing in their seats climbing to a cruising altitude of 30,000 feet and heading southbound to Sydney. Creed had donned his headset and was fumbling on the armrest as he searched for the rock music channel and volume controls. Boston-Wright placed a pillow against the window and tried to get some shuteye. There was obviously going to be little or no conversation on this flight but that suited her. She had a restless night's sleep and craved a few winks.

Creed continued to fidget, pressing the controls on the dividing armrest and popping his headset on and off, giving Boston-Wright little opportunity to sleep. She finally gave up and was thankful when the air hostess arrived with a muffin and coffee.

"So, sir, do you think we'll get any closer with Mick Darlington being our man?" she asked, although not in a confirming way.

Creed gave her a look as to why she doubted that Darlington was their man. He pulled the inflight magazine out of the seat pocket and started thumbing through it without responding to Boston-Wright.

An hour and ten minutes later, their flight landed in Sydney. Creed and Boston-Wright were exiting the terminal and climbing into a taxi, heading to their hotel.

"The Holiday Inn, Potts Point," Creed instructed the turban-wearing, Indian taxi driver, who gave Creed a wry smile as he changed lanes without indicating and passed through the traffic lights while turning red. Jack was convinced the driver had gotten his license from a Corn Flakes packet and decided to tighten his seatbelt for the hairy twenty minute ride.

The Holiday Inn was positioned on the bend of busy Darlinghurst Road and was more Kings Cross than Potts Point. A few shady characters sat on park benches across from the hotel and a couple of girls of the night were out early, trying their luck with the lunchtime crowd. The hotel was close to the police station on Elizabeth Bay Road where they were to have a meeting with Detective Chris Towbridge. Hopefully, he could shed some light on a couple of murders of prostitutes in the area, possibly around the time of Darlington doing some work in Sydney.

There was no time for lunch. Boston-Wright grabbed a packet of salt n vinegar chips from her room and devoured most of them before the lift hit the ground floor. Creed was already outside hailing a taxi. Boston-Wright slid into the plastic covered back seat of the cab as Creed followed her, giving the driver the address. Her look indicated she thought the plastic was a bit odd until Creed explained it was done so the cab could be hosed out if a drunk threw up all over the seat. The driver looked into the rearview mirror, nodded and smiled as he carved his way through the back streets of the Cross, like Mark Webber at Monaco. Boston-Wright looked out the window, her body tossed from side to side like she was riding the Twister at a fairground amusement park, passing countless graffiti-walled buildings, before finally arriving at the station.

Chris Towbridge was exactly like he sounded. His slightly effeminate voice complemented his blond tips on his well-styled hair, his uniform neatly pressed and his shoes polished to a high gloss. Even his desk spoke efficiency. There was just one file on top, albeit a thick one.

"Welcome, Detectives. Can I organize you both some coffee?" Towbridge asked warmly.

"That would be great," Boston-Wright replied, cut short by Jack's non-acceptance and lingering stare. She was unfazed.

Towbridge produced a photo of Sally Carter, an aboriginal prostitute, 27, killed in a back street off Darlinghurst Road. Like the northern New South Wales murders, Sally had her hands bound behind her back with Smith & Wesson handcuffs. Her throat had been slit.

"Any suspects? The girl's pimp?" Creed asked.

"No, Tommy had a couple of witnesses' accounts for his whereabouts on the night. Ironically, he was found dead about hundred meters from Sally three weeks later. Heroin overdose," Towbridge replied scratching his chin. "Nope, we came up empty-handed on Sally. No witnesses. No sightings of a car, nothing."

"Who identified Sally's body?" Boston-Wright asked.

"Her mother. She got quite a shock," Towbridge recalled. "She thought Sally was nursing. Never knew she was on the game."

Creed tossed over a photo of Mick Darlington to Towbridge, who picked it up and donned a pair of Dolce & Gabbana reading glasses to take a closer look. "No, can't say I know this man. He's not on our radar, Detective." Creed felt a little deflated. An afternoon had gone by and they were no closer to solving their crimes as when they boarded their morning flight.

Towbridge offered to drop Creed and Boston-Wright back to the hotel, passing the site where Sally's body was found. It was ten to seven as they cruised up Darlinghurst Road. Night was just starting to fall and the streets were becoming more active, although the real action didn't start till after ten, so Towbridge assured his passengers, giving Boston-Wright a playful wink.

"We'll drop you back at the hotel, Boston-Wright. Detective Towbridge and I are going to check out the area and grab a bite to eat." Creed turned to his fellow officer, dismissing her for the night without an invite to join them.

Initially, Boston-Wright was pissed off, but once back at the hotel, she felt relieved. She ordered room service and ran a hot bath. She would've liked to have been included but her body appreciated the warm bath salts, and the chicken Caesar salad hit the right spot. An early night in bed wouldn't go astray.

Creed, on the other hand, was on a mission to get absorbed in everything Kings Cross. Towbridge thought he was taking his research a little too far. After five bars and ten pints of beer, Towbridge finally convinced Creed to settle down at the Bourbon & Beef and partake in some dinner. The restaurant was renowned for their 400g rib eye fillet steaks, having won many Sydney restaurant awards. Hungry and tired from being dragged from bar to bar, Towbridge was relieved when Creed agreed to eat.

Towbridge greeted the maître de with a hug and was shown along with Creed to the best table in the restaurant, a window seat overlooking the street. The restaurant was busy for a mid-week night, mainly supported by well-dressed men that gave rise to Creed thinking his fellow officer batted for the other team. Jack cleared his throat a few times, each time a little deeper and louder trying to indicate to all and sundry that he was not of 'that' persuasion as he read the menu while a softly spoken waiter poured the ice water and placed a basket of fresh bread on the table. Towbridge sensed Creed's lack of comfort and smiled to himself. At least his liver could recuperate over dinner.

****

A door slammed so hard, it was surprising it stayed on its hinges. Boston-Wright sat up in bed, startled and dazed, as she heard keys being tossed onto a table in the adjoining room and the sound of a toilet flushing. It was 2.30am and Creed was home. She dropped back onto her pillow and looked skyward to the ceiling, cursing Creed for waking her up. She rolled onto her right side, punching her pillow as she tried to get comfortable and get back off to sleep. A few more tosses and she finally succumbed.

The alarm on her iPhone roared at 6.30am, almost making Boston-Wright jump out of her skin. She was in a deep sleep, although feeling a little drained thanks to Creed's early morning arrival. She jumped under a piping hot shower to fully wake herself, got dressed and was knocking on Creed's door by 7am.

Jack greeted Jo wearing just a towel hanging from his hips. His grey chest hair was a welcome change from the waxed men she had dated. She dropped

133

her eyes to the floor and asked if he was coming downstairs for breakfast.

"Just coffee for me, love. I'll see you at the rental car desk at 8," Creed replied, leaning on the door arch, with one hand holding a cup of coffee.

****

The rental car assistant handed the keys to Boston-Wright after Creed feverishly waved that he was not today's driver and pointed to the Hyundai in the car park. While Boston-Wright adjusted her seat, checked her side mirrors and adjusted the rear view mirror, Creed keyed in the address on his iPhone for the Parramatta CID, which was about an hour's drive away, thankfully against peak hour traffic.

Boston-Wright ambled the compact Hyundai i30 down Darlinghurst Road, into William Street. then onto the Western Arterial Road. Creed, still recovering from the night before, reclined his seat and closed his eyes.

"Bit of a late night, sir?" Boston-Wright cheekily enquired, smiling but keeping her eyes firmly on the traffic in front of her.

"I was working, Boston-Wright."

"Of course, sir. Right up to 2.30am this morning."

Creed rolled his head to the right and cocked his sunglasses to give Boston-Wright a glare through his bloodshot eyes.

"That's when all the hookers come out, my dear. I showed Darlington's photo around."

"And?" Boston-Wright replied with anticipation.

"No luck. But I still think he's our man."

"I'm not seeing it, sir. Even Towbridge couldn't add any strength to your suspicions," Boston-Wright replied.

"He's been in an area, left, and then a few days later we've found a dead body. An aboriginal girl, handcuffed and brutally murdered," Creed expressed with in a firm and forthright tone.

"All except for Sam Thompson. He was male," Boston-Wright responded.

"Well, if it's not Darlington, then this whole exercise has been a fucking waste of time," Creed commented, replacing his sunglasses and turning away from his driver.

But Creed couldn't let it rest. "Seriously, do you think I'm wrong about Darlington?"

"Thompson doesn't fit, sir. I think we may be too focused on one tree rather than the whole forest,"

Boston-Wright replied as she looked at the road signs directing her toward the exit for Parramatta, indicating as she crossed lanes.

"You don't give up, do you, Boston-Wright? You're just like your old man."

"Thank you, sir. I'll take that as a compliment." She gave Creed a broad smile as she careered down the exit ramp toward Parramatta's CBD.

CHAPTER 11

Their first meeting wasn't until three, so Creed and Boston-Wright had a few hours to kill. It was too early to check into the Parramatta Park Royal. It was a pity, as Creed dreamt of more sleep but Boston-Wright was keen to relax at the poolside bar, kick back with a couple of drinks and have an early lunch.

Boston-Wright looked at the inviting water and wished she had brought her swimmers. Creed was oblivious to the water and had his eyes fixated on the thirty-something blonde on the lazy boy at the other end of the pool, his attention not unnoticed by Boston-Wright, who thought it was probably just as well she had forgotten her bathers.

After lunch, Creed and Boston-Wright checked into the hotel, quickly unpacked and met back in the lobby by 2.00pm. Jack wanted to call into the Dad's Army office on route to Parramatta CID.

The Dad's Army office was located on the fourth floor of a modest six story building in a side street off Parramatta Road. The lift shook and reeked of mildew and both Creed and Boston-Wright were glad the doors finally opened on the fourth floor. The receptionist announced their arrival to the manager before she showed them down the narrow, dark corridor to his office. The manager, who had now taken a phone call, waved the detectives into his office, gesturing for them to take a seat on the sofa.

"Yes, I know you are on the pension, love, but our rate is $49 an hour. You won't find it any cheaper, not with the quality we offer. I'll place you on hold and Miss Jones can book you in.

"Christ, these old biddies want to rob you blind," the manager sighed. "Now what can I do for you two?"

"Charlie Warburton, your man up there in the Tweed, said you could help us," Creed replied, hoping that a bit of name dropping may hold them in good stead for their unscheduled visit. The manager nodded as he took a sip of his coffee.

"You had a fierce electrical storm here in Sydney in February. I believe Parramatta was particularly badly hit," Creed explained.

"It was a ripper, Detective. Roofs were ripped off, homes were flooded and trees were uprooted everywhere. A bloody mess it was," the manager recalled.

"We understand that you had to get extra help to do the repairs," Creed stated. Producing Darlington's photo from his suit jacket pocket, Creed asked, "Did you have a Mick Darlington working for you during that period?"

Dave Hamilton, the Dad's Army manager, scratched his head and took a closer look at Creed's photo. He didn't look like the sharpest tool in the shed as he started to fumble on the keyboard of his desktop computer, cursing as he typed with a single finger.

"Yep, he was here with his lovely wife, Kay. We had her on cleaning duties as well."

"Any chance we could get a printout of the dates and jobs he did for you?" Boston-Wright asked.

"Sure. I remember them now. I remember how strange it was that they stayed in a van park," Hamilton remarked.

"And what's so strange about that?" Boston-Wright asked.

"The van park was in Potts Point, which is about an

hour's drive from here," Hamilton replied with a smirk on his face as he grabbed the job schedule off the printer.

"Maybe Michael enjoyed a rub n tug on Darlinghurst Road," Hamilton commented with a cheeky grin like a 12 year old school boy. Creed grabbed the notes, thanked Hamilton and made his way to the office door.

"Aren't you going to tell me what this is about? There's not a dodgy work claim coming, is there?"

"Just a general enquiry, Mr. Hamilton. Thank you." Boston-Wright raced to catch up with Creed, who was holding the lift door open.

Once back at the car, Creed had a change of plans. "Let's head back to the Potts Point caravan park and see if the manager there can tell us anything about the Darlington's. Boston-Wright pulled into the late afternoon traffic and headed back to Potts Point. The traffic was more congested than their morning ride and drivers seemed not to understand how to use their indicators when changing lanes.

The entrance to the van park was calming, a wide open entry with royal palms defining the roadway to the reception. A water fountain just inside the gate gave the place a resort feeling as Boston-Wright observed the 10klm/hour drive to the manager's hut. The duty manager greeted his new guests, but upon discovering they were with the police, his tone soon cooled.

Words like privacy and confidentiality were bandied around, only irritating Creed further. He explained that the assistant manager would be helping their enquiries and closed with an alternative scenario that he could return with the Potts Point Police in several squad cars to collect the information he needed. A printout of the stay of the Darlington's was produced immediately. Creed and Boston-Wright joined the long queue back to Parramatta.

While Boston-Wright battled the traffic, Creed skipped through the printout. It showed the Darlington's spent five weeks at the van park from early February to mid-March, the period between the Tweed murders and when Sally Carter was killed in Amos Lane, Potts Point.

"We are getting close, Boston-Wright," Creed let out with enthusiasm, flicking the page with his right index finger.

"That's great, sir. I'm starving. I need to eat when we get back," Boston-Wright replied, rubbing her stomach, trying to fight off the hunger pangs.

"Let's celebrate, Boston-Wright. Madame Wong's is

the most exclusive Chinese restaurant in Sydney and it's not far from our hotel. Let me make a booking," Creed remarked, fumbling for his phone inside his jacket.

"Actually, sir, I haven't brought any fancy clothes with me. Can we just eat in the hotel? I'm bushed anyway."

****

After a quick freshen up, Boston-Wright waited in the lobby for Creed. The lift doors opened and he appeared. Crisp white shirt, open neck, freshly shaven and hair slicked back. Creed scrubbed up pretty well with just twenty minutes preparation. With his arm cocked, Creed indicated to Boston-Wright to link arms as he escorted her to Tony's Grille, the hotel's premier restaurant. Creed was obviously in high spirits and Boston-Wright appreciated the extra attention. It had been a while since any man had shown her attention, even if this was from her boss.

The maître de showed them to a window table. Even though it was dark, the work colleagues had a nice view to the pool, which looked inviting. The gardens were flood lit. Creed seemed more relaxed, perhaps more confident after today's meetings. For once he seemed to show some interest in Boston-Wright and her life.

"Do you ever feel under pressure to live up to your father's name?" he asked.

"Sometimes. He was a great role model, and yes, I'd like to be as good as him one day," Boston-Wright replied.

She was impressed that Creed was showing an interest. She decided to open up a little more and talk about her early days in Robbery and what it was like growing up as a copper's daughter. Feeling more relaxed, Boston-Wright tossed in a few questions to Creed.

"Your daughter needs medical assistance, Jack?"

"Yes, Jo. She suffered at school from a bully, which she's carried on to her later teens. She gets quite depressed, sometimes suicidal. She lives for most of the year at New Farm Clinic. It's a mental health facility in Brisbane. That's why my family still lives in Brisbane. It's not by choice," Creed recalls with a sad look gripping his face. Boston-Wright's heart strings were heavily tugged.

Dinner ended with a coffee poolside. It had been a pleasant night. Jo felt a bit more comfortable with Creed and her position on the team. Everything was quiet back in Kingscliff, as they hadn't received any updates from Pratt or Smith, indicating the investigation was stalling or perhaps the mice were playing while the cat was away. In any case, Boston-Wright hoped this wouldn't affect Creed's mood, although she had witnessed some pretty low lows with him.

The ride up to their rooms was quiet. Creed seemed to have drifted back into work mode. His mind was clearly elsewhere as he bid Boston-Wright goodnight. She watched as he fumbled, tapping his keycard on the reader three times before the light finally turned green and he was inside. Boston-Wright entered her room and smiled, wondering if she would have keycard issues when she hit her mid-fifties. She had 20 years to go yet.

****

Breakfast arrived at 7.15am, half an hour late. Boston-Wright sighed as her orange juice was now tomato, the bacon was cold and the eggs were fried and not scrambled. But there was no time to complain and re-order. Checkout was at 8am.

The old Creed had returned by the time Boston-Wright hit the lobby. The charming, empathetic man she had dinner with the night before had morphed back into the grumpy old Creed she had become accustomed to over the past few months. He looked like he had the weight of the world on his shoulders. Boston-Wright rolled her eyes, knowing the trip to the airport in peak hour traffic was going to be murder, especially with Captain Gloomy in the passenger seat.

Check-in was hectic. Creed's lack of patience showed up when he tried to automatically check in, cursing the machine and bellowing for assistance from an airline staff member. The Qantas staffer calmly checked Creed in and sent him on his way with a smile, most likely faked.

Boston-Wright was impressed with the Qantas Club Lounge in Sydney. It was far grander than Coolangatta and the clientele were more businesslike, not so many of the yellow shirt mining brigade. Maybe a happy hunting ground for a new husband, Boston-Wright thought, although it was unlikely she would be returning any time soon.

Cred was in a reflective mood. He sipped his coffee and looked into space. Boston-Wright could see the cogs of his mind doing overtime.

"You seem to be a bit distant this morning, Jack. Everything okay?" Boston-Wright enquired with one eye on a thirty-something businessman in a dark navy pinstripe suit, carrying a leather briefcase, striding by and wishing she was engaged in more than conversation with him. A wedding band on his left hand caught her eye and brought her back to reality and to Creed.

"We just seem to be going around in circles. Darlington has been around in each of these murders but nobody can ID him."

"Our break will come soon. Maybe when we land in Brisbane," Boston-Wright replied, throwing in a bit of optimism and hoping to lift the mood.

"And Pratt called me last night. He's resigning at the end of the case. That's all I fucking need," Creed sighed.

The hour and ten minute flight to Brisbane was bumpy. The plane ran into a few electrical storms over Newcastle, causing Boston-Wright to grip onto her partner's arm like a crocodile going in for a death roll. Creed flexed his forearm upon landing, trying to get the circulation back into the muscle, relieved the flight was over.

The reception of the Brisbane Hilton felt like a second home for Boston-Wright, having been there recently. The Duty Manager gave her a broad smile and welcomed her back. Twenty minutes later,

Creed and Boston-Wright were on the Elizabeth Street taxi rank, climbing into a yellow cab and heading to the Dad's Army office at Springwood.

Keith Winchester welcomed the detectives to the business and took them into his office. After explaining they were conducting some general enquiries around Mick Darlington, Winchester ran a report showing the times when Darlington had worked with the agency over the past eighteen months. Armed with the printout, Creed and Boston-Wright returned to the Hilton.

"Can I leave this file with you tonight, Jo? I'm going to have some quality time with the family. Melissa's home, so we want to have a roast for dinner," Creed stated, handing the file to Boston-Wright as he stepped off the pavement into a VW Golf, driven by his wife. Boston-Wright smiled, took the file and bent over to peer through the car window, expecting Creed to introduce her. But all she got was a wave as the car pulled out into Elizabeth Street and punched its way into the peak hour traffic.

As she entered the lift to take her to the Club floor, the upgrade courtesy of the Duty Manager, Boston-Wright recalled that Mrs. Creed looked washed out, her face drawn, skin dry and her hair not brushed. But with the last five years of living hell, how else was the woman to look?

Boston-Wright washed away the day with complimentary champagne and hors d'oeuvres and took in the sunset over Brisbane. The Club Lounge was relatively quiet. An elderly couple sat next to the window looking toward the Brisbane River, deeply engrossed in each other's conversation. Boston-Wright smiled as the old man patted his wife on the knee before wandering off to refill her glass. The lady caught Jo staring and gave her a warm smile. Boston-Wright returned the smile and drifted off with thoughts of whether she would ever be sitting happily in the Club Lounge with her true love when she would be in her seventies. The love game to date hadn't been kind, and with that, Boston-Wright gulped the last of her champagne and withdrew to her room.

At 9.40pm, the in-room phone rang. Boston-Wright, who had slipped into a daze while watching a re-run of Midsomer Murders, almost jumped out of her skin as she scampered across the room to her bedside table.

"Is he with you?" the male voice asked.

"No, Pratt. Jack's at home with his wife," Boston-Wright replied. "Why?"

"I've been ringing his mobile for the last hour. We've got another murder down here."

CHAPTER 12

Boston-Wright sat on the end of the bed in shock. She couldn't believe her ears. She might have been dozing ten minutes ago, but now she was wide awake. She picked up the phone and dialed 7, the in-room dining. She ordered a hot chocolate with extra marshmallows and then got talked into a slice of the cake of the day, Bavarian Black Forest. It wasn't her favourite but she thought it would help out the Philippine lady taking her order. Boston-Wright thought she was doing her Good Samaritan deed of the day, hoping to herself that this late night cake binge would not stay on her hips.

Boston-Wright hit the redial button on her iPhone. This time it was ringing. Creed must have finally got off the phone.

"Did Pratt get hold of you, sir?" Boston-Wright enquired, still in shock but also conscious she was interrupting the boss on one of his rare nights at home.

"Yes, yes. I've heard the news."

"Any more details?"

"Same as the other scenarios. Coloured girl, hands behind her back and throat slit. She's probably been dead a week to ten days. But it may not be related to the others."

"O'Halloran wants us back tonight but he can get fucked. We'll leave early in the morning. Good night, Boston-Wright."

Boston-Wright clicked the end button and tossed the phone back on the bed, thinking Creed ended the call rather formally. Maybe his wife was close by, she thought. A knock at the door announced the arrival of the hot chocolate and black forest cake. It would be her sleeping pill tonight.

****

Creed and Boston-Wright drove out of the Hertz rental lounge at 6.30am and merged into the traffic on George Street before exiting onto the freeway heading south down the coast to Kingscliff. While Boston-Wright drove, Creed looked through the paperwork Winchester provided on Darlington.

Puffing and blowing, Creed closed the file and looked out the window.

"Crazy I know, sir," Boston-Wright commented as she looked at the bumper to bumper traffic entering Brisbane.

"What?" Creed came back from his thoughts to align with Boston-Wright's comment.

"I thought you were puffing about the non-moving traffic going the other way," Boston-Wright replied.

"No. It's the bloody case."

"Are you going cool on Darlington?" she asked.

"I can't put my finger on it, but there's something. Something isn't right," Creed said, dropping the file on the floor under his legs.

The rest of the car ride to Kingscliff was solemn. Both realized the case was stalling and that O'Halloran would have their guts for garters, especially now that they've run up more expenses in Sydney and Brisbane. Pulling into the parking lot of the Station, Creed suggested that Boston-Wright drop the rental car back to the depot and take the rest of the day off. He would deal with O'Halloran on his own.

Greg Pratt was the first of the crew to wander into Creed's office. Creed was slumped in his office chair, a fair indication of how he was feeling about the case.

"Get anything in Sydney, Jack?" Pratt asked.

"Not really. Yes, Darlington was in the area during the times those poor girls were murdered but nobody could ID his car or him," Creed replied, pulling receipts from his suit jacket and tossing them on the table. "I'm getting the feeling I might have cocked up here." He sighed, giving Pratt a lingering stare, hoping for some recompense. Pratt never uttered a word.

****

Boston-Wright put a load of washing on and did some light tidying of her house. Even though she had been away for the past three days, she was not tempted to cook herself a home meal. Instead she placed the Papa Giuseppe frozen lasagna into the microwave and keyed in three minutes thirty seconds. She poured herself a glass of red and took up a prime position in front of the television. A re-run of Inspector Lynley would be the closest thing to company she would have tonight.

Boston-Wright arrived at the station at 7.45am the next morning. Creed was already in. He was clean-shaven, wearing a fresh shirt, Boss jeans and a black

Versace jacket, but he looked like shit. It looked like he had been on an all-night bender.

Boston-Wright looked at Creed's office, hoping to get a welcoming hello. But nothing. His head was buried in a mountain of paperwork, including receipts from their trip. Boston-Wright threw her bag on the floor next to her desk and slumped down into her chair. Her desk was covered in a pile of paperwork that had mounted up over the past few days while she was in Sydney. The thought of clearing the backlog temporarily overwhelmed her. Creed called her into his office.

"Here are my expenses. Check them over, add yours in and hand the whole thing to Accounts. See if they can get the money back into our banks in the next pay run," Creed explained, handing his receipts over to Boston-Wright and greeting her with a numb look.

Boston-Wright started sorting through the files on her desk placing them in priority of urgency. She took her expense receipts and placed them into Creed's folder and left it on her desk. The edges of a couple of photos caught her eye as they protruded from one of the many files on her desk.

Boston-Wright looked over the notes of the Jessica Campbell case while glancing at the photos that first caught her attention. She tossed the file onto the pile and quickly grabbed another case, feverishly thumbing through the notes. Then she looked at the Berg file.

Boston-Wright gathered the case files and raced into Creed's office, looking like she had just discovered an anomaly in Creed's accounts. Creed picked up on the look and wondered if she had spotted the porno movie rental on the hotel bill.

"Sir, we are looking for the wrong guy," Boston-Wright gasped, much to Creed's relief.

"What do you mean, Boston-Wright?"

"We know Darlington drives a white Toyota Land Cruiser. A similar car was seen in the vicinity of the Bear Club on the night Sam Thompson was murdered. But there's no mention of a Land Cruiser in any of the other case files. However, there is mention of a Nissan Patrol being seen in the area in three of the other cases. We're looking for the wrong guy, sir."

"But remember when we spoke to Darlington in Casino?" Creed carefully said, choosing his words slowly.

"Yes, sort of," Boston-Wright replied.

"I complimented him on owning a Land Cruiser and he replied that he had only owned the vehicle for about six months," Creed explained, looking to see if the wheels of thought were turning in Boston-Wright's brain.

"Meaning?"

"Meaning we need to run a check on what car Mr. Darlington owned before the Land Cruiser," Creed replied with a smug look.

Boston-Wright called the Department of Transport and after validating her credentials, she asked for a check on vehicle registrations owned by Mick Darlington over the past three years. The lady on the other end of the line immediately confirmed his ownership of a white Toyota Land Cruiser, but nothing else. When Boston-Wright pressed the lady further, she still came up empty.

It didn't make sense. How could there be no records of vehicle registration to Mick Darlington prior to his current four wheel drive? Boston-Wright was rattled. She sat back in her chair, staring into space while keeping the registration clerk holding on the line. As Darlington had been a normal working man all his life, there would be no reason to register a vehicle in a company name. Boston-Wright asked if the clerk could search by street name.

"Yes, Detective. I have a Nissan Patrol registered to a Kay Darlington of that same address."

Boston-Wright could hardly contain her excitement. She raced back into Creed's office, closed the door and raised her hand for a high five.

"Bingo! Kay Darlington owned a Nissan Patrol up until about six months ago," Boston-Wright spat out with a grin from ear to ear as she slapped Creed's hand.

"Get him in. Not her, just him. And Boston-Wright, we need to do this by the book. Give him the option to bring his solicitor," Creed replied, clasping his hands and tapping them rapidly on the desk.

Darlington was surprisingly calm when Boston-Wright phoned. He agreed to come into the station at 3.30pm today. He never really asked what it was about and confirmed that his solicitor would not be attending. Boston-Wright hung up thinking Darlington was one cool customer, putting it down to his military career.

****

Mick Darlington sat calmly in the interview room sipping his Earl Grey tea waiting for the detectives to arrive. He wore khaki trousers, a white polo and slip-on brown shoes. His almost white hair had been recently cut and his beard trimmed.

Creed and Boston-Wright entered the room in unison, pulling back their chairs to take up their position opposite Darlington, who greeted them with a smile and eye contact. Boston-Wright glanced at Creed, raising her eyebrow, acknowledging Darlington's coolness. Darlington didn't miss it. Creed undid his jacket button while Boston-Wright sorted her notes on Darlington's vehicle registrations.

"You're Bruno Boston's daughter, right?" Darlington asked of Boston-Wright.

"Yes, that's right."

"He and your mother lived just outside Bangalow, if I remember rightly. I used to pass their home on my way to Canungra when I was in the Army," Darlington commented, trying to make light conversation. But Boston-Wright wasn't interested in conversation and immediately took back control by starting the questions about the vehicle registration, the reason as to why Darlington was here. Jack looked impressed.

"Records show us that you drive a Toyota Land Cruiser," Boston-Wright stated, getting a nod from Darlington.

"But your previous vehicle, a Nissan Patrol, was registered in your wife's name. Why was that?"

Boston-Wright asked, as she shuffled some papers on the interview table.

"Kay is five years older than me and we thought that as she was getting older we may have some trouble in her renewing her driver's license and maybe registering the car," Darlington coolly replied, sitting crossed-legged, his arms folded on his right thigh. His eyes shifted from Creed back to Boston-Wright.

"And do you still have the Patrol now, Mr. Darlington?" Creed asked.

"No, Detective Sergeant. It is Sergeant, not Inspector, right?" Darlington commented looking Creed in the face with his head slightly cocked to the left, trying to throw the detective off his game.

"The vehicle was stolen and your Pottsville boys found it trashed in scrub," Darlington said. "A couple of aboriginal kids supposedly but nobody was ever charged. That Father Douglas stuck up for them in court and the case was thrown out for lack of evidence, I believe."

Boston-Wright wound up the interview, noted to call the Pottsville Station and thanked Darlington for his co-operation. Creed shook his head and slovenly walked back to his office, complementing Boston-Wright on her interview and rewarding her with an early night. But there was no rest for Creed. This case was beating him.

****

Boston-Wright took advantage of an early night to catch up on some sleep and hit the sack at 9.05pm. She was lulled into a deep sleep thinking about her parents and the fun times she had living in the family home near Bangalow.

The phone rang. Boston-Wright almost jumped out of her skin. She sat up in bed, startled, trying to work out if the house phone was really ringing or if she was just dreaming. She rubbed her eyes hard, shook her head and threw back the covers as she raced into the lounge, fumbling for the light switch.

"Hello?"

There was no answer. Just silence.

"Hello? Who is this?" Boston-Wright asked as she looked into the kitchen. The wall clock said 10.15pm.

After a few more seconds of waiting, Boston-Wright hung up. She was now fully awake and a little rattled. She dialed the recall button, but no number appeared. Who the hell would be ringing her on the house phone at 10.15, she wondered? It couldn't be anyone from the station, as they would have rung her mobile.

Creed is kind of an early-to-bed, early-to-rise kind of bloke, except when he's researching for a case. And then she had a spooky thought.

Mick Darlington.

She tried to think how he could have gotten her number as the kettle boiled the water for her chamomile tea. She gathered her cup and sat on the lounge, her knees under her chin, while she sipped her drink. She was worried but determined not to let this rattle her.

CHAPTER 13

Boston-Wright walked briskly into Creed's office the following morning, closing the door and pulling out a chair in front of his desk. She looked rattled and Creed picked up on it.

"What's up, Boston-Wright? You okay?" Creed asked with a curious look on his face. The blood had drained a little from Boston-Wright's face, making her look whiter than normal, almost sickly.

"I had a strange call last night on the home phone," Boston-Wright replied, fidgeting in her seat and picking her nails at the same time.

"And who was it?" Creed asked.

"The person didn't speak. It was silent. I couldn't help think that Darlington made a comment about our family home that afternoon. Then I get a prank call."

"Do you want me to arrange a trace?" Creed offered.

"I don't think the call wasn't long enough to get a trace, but you could try. It just rattled me a little. I've never had prank calls before," Boston-Wright replied, her voice jittery.

Pratt knocked on the door and barged in, thereby ending the private conversation between Boston-Wright and Creed. Boston-Wright could have done with a bit more time. It may have given her some reassurances and perhaps settled her nerves but that opportunity had gone.

"I spoke to a mate of mine, a psychologist by trade, who's done a bit of profiling for the boys in Sydney," Pratt went on. "I spoke to him about our victims and he's come back with a rough sketch of the type of person we may be looking for."

"Interesting," Creed replied, looking at Pratt's notebook as he opened it and was about to give an outline.

"Okay, it's hard to determine if our killer is a serial killer," Pratt started with the summary. Boston-Wright and Creed listened attentively. Boston-Wright was impressed with Pratt's last rush of enthusiasm, especially for a copper who was about to retire. Maybe he wanted to go out with a bang.

"A person who commits a number of murders over

a period of time is patient and organized," Pratt continued.

That certainly fits the profile of Mick Darlington. Here was a man who spent most of his life in the armed services, used to discipline and most likely well-organized. He's probably built up a good skill in being patient, something enhanced as he retired and started doing skilled labor jobs with Dad's Army. Some of his work had been quite intricate, again requiring patience.

"Killing is not the main game. It's just a byproduct of control," Pratt stated.

Darlington was certainly a controlling person, as both Creed and Boston-Wright had observed, especially with his wife. She looked positively scared of her husband. Both detectives determined that the marriage would most likely be a loveless one, despite being in their later years. Creed recalled their visit to the Casino caravan park where Mrs. Darlington was sent to the shops to get supplies and Darlington was most edgy that she had not returned within a specified time period. It was as if she had been let off a leash and should have returned.

Creed asked that with all the female victims having had recent sexual activity, would sex be a major driver in such a person.

"Only as a way to express control," Pratt advised. "Lustful sex, kinky sex maybe as an outlet to some aggression but certainly not love." The no love bit seemed to fit with Darlington. However, it could not be determined if Darlington had sex with any of the victims. Creed leaned back in his chair, his hands interlocked behind his head as he thought over what Pratt was saying.

Pratt continued reading from his notes. "These types of killers outwardly exhibit calmness but underneath they have a fire of aggression they try to keep in check." Darlington would fit the bill, although they had not seen any aggression.

Another trait Pratt shared was that such killers have an underlying trigger; something deep-seated that set them off on their killing way. In the case of the Tweed Coast victims, they are all black, mostly aboriginal, except for the Afro-American tourist Sharon Berg. All female except for Tom Langley, who was Darlene Ferguson's pimp come boyfriend. Perhaps the killer hates aboriginal women?

But Sam Thompson is wrong. Yes, he was black but he was male. There was no sexual activity with him but his murder was the most violent, tortured, leg broken, stabbed and then doused in petrol and set alight. In some ways it would seem Sam was a mistake. Perhaps the killer was at their breaking point.

Boston-Wright and Creed thanked Pratt for the insights his friend gave them. They concluded that they were still on the right track in pursuing Darlington. Boston-Wright suggested she should make a visit to Darlington's house alone and ask him some more questions. Boston-Wright was convinced it was Darlington who had made the prank call the night before; perhaps she could get him freely talking without Creed being around.

"Maybe he called to have a chat the other night and then froze before hanging up. You will recall both he and his wife were quite charming to me when we searched the house, showing me family photos and snaps of when he was in the Army," Boston-Wright commented.

"Yes, that's true. Maybe you could draw him out further," Creed said, rubbing his right hand through his hair and ending in a sigh.

"But whatever you do, Boston-Wright, you must be on guard at all times. He may be letting you into his world but these killers have no regard for life. You are disposable," Creed reminded her, sending a chill down her spine.

The two detectives tossed around some ideas on

how to approach Darlington. He must not be suspicious about being interviewed. Rather, Boston-Wright was popping in for a chat. If it felt formal or something premeditated, Darlington would clam up and not speak freely. The invitation to meet would need to sound special, even personal.

Boston-Wright and Creed worked on a phone script. It was decided that Boston-Wright would call at around 6 o'clock and say she was on her way home, asking if she could drop off some items the team collected during the search. The tone needed to be carefree, almost a throwaway conversation. But she needed to show empathy. The items she was returning were no longer needed for the investigation but she realized their personal importance to Mick Darlington and his wife. She wanted to personally deliver them back to their family home.

Creed was nervous. Nervous for where the case was heading and nervous for Boston-Wright. She was putting her life at risk. If Darlington smelt a rat, Boston-Wright could be in serious trouble. Creed reminded Boston-Wright that under no circumstances was she to go anywhere with Mr. Darlington alone. It would be preferable that Kay Darlington is at home when she popped around.

Perhaps she could try to find that out when she phoned Darlington later. A comment about sampling another slice of Kay's famous lemon crunch pie could be weaved into the conversation.

While Boston-Wright tossed some ideas around on her notepad, Creed phoned O'Halloran upstairs, seeking more resources. He gave the Chief Super a snapshot of where the investigation was and that he felt confident they were getting closer to an arrest. An imminent arrest pleased O'Halloran until Creed sprang the idea of more overtime for a few of the lads to act as surveillance for Boston-Wright while she was in with Darlington. Somebody needed to be close just in case things went wrong. O'Halloran granted Creed some more overtime but reminded him of how much this case was costing and that they needed an arrest soon.

Creed called a few of his most trusted officers into his office and explained what was about to go down. He needed his best and most alert officers on the surveillance roster tonight, as they were protecting one of their own. As Creed wound up the brief, he looked through the venetian blinds in his office out to Boston-Wright sitting at her desk. She may have been the newest and least qualified member to the murder squad but she was growing in importance with spades. He felt like a father figure to her, in some ways a job passed onto him by his former colleague Bruno Boston. He liked the role.

Boston-Wright practiced her script, occasionally glancing up at the wall clock. At precisely 6 o'clock, she looked over at Creed, took a deep breath, turned her chair toward a blank wall and dialed Darlington. The call connected and Mick Darlington answered.

In her most calming voice, Boston-Wright offered to drop some items off to Darlington's house on her way home. To be more convincing, she even lowered her voice occasionally to give the impression that what she was doing was a secret but she wanted the Darlington's to have their personal possessions returned immediately.

Mick Darlington was polite in inviting Boston-Wright to stay for dinner with both he and his wife. The knowledge that Kay Darlington would be home gave Boston-right some sense of relief. The visit was set.

CHAPTER 14

Boston-Wright arrived at the Darlington's at around 6.40pm. The sun was just going down as two little kids riding their bikes down the street responded to their mother's call and went home. Boston-Wright grabbed the plastic bag containing the Darlington's possessions from the front seat, looked at herself in the rearview mirror, tidied her hair and got out of the car.

Mick Darlington was standing at the front door to welcome her as she walked up the driveway. She looked toward the ground as she went over in her mind the schooling she had from Creed in the afternoon, taking deep breaths as she walked. She gave Mr. Darlington a smile as he pushed open the fly screen door and gestured for her to enter the lounge room.

"Kay, Detective Boston-Wright is here," Mick Darlington called out to his wife.

"Jo, please, Mr. Darlington," Boston-Wright replied, remembering Pratt's conversation to make the discussion less formal.

"Jo it is, on the proviso you call us Mick and Kay," Mick said as Mrs. Darlington appeared in the room, wiping her hands on an apron attached around her waist.

"Now, would you like a beer or wine?" Darlington asked as Boston-Wright sat down on the two seater sofa facing the door. "I take it you are off duty now."

"A beer would be good, thanks," Boston-Wright replied while looking at Mrs. Darlington, who was going to fetch the drinks. Mick Darlington locked the screen door but kept the main door open, much to the relief of Boston-Wright, even though she was now locked in.

Mrs. Darlington returned to the lounge with two stubbies of Tooheys, glasses, a white wine and a bowl of cashew nuts. Mick Darlington picked up a glass, angled it and slowly poured the ice cold beer into it, creating a decent head before handing over the glass to Boston-Wright.

"You've done that before," Boston-Wright remarked as she toasted the Darlington's with, "Cheers."

Mick Darlington was dressed in brown shorts and a beige polo shirt and looked relaxed as he sat back into his Jason recliner rocking chair while Kay sat in the other recliner but looked edgy as she sipped her chardonnay.

"Now, before we get started," Darlington stated, "I hope you will stay for dinner. It's nothing much. A beef curry but Kay does a good one. She learnt the recipe when we lived in Malaysia when I was in the Army. About the only good thing we got from those little black bastards."

Kay dipped her head and took another sip. Boston-Wright wasn't sure if she was embarrassed by Mick's promotion of her Beef Tikka Marsala or his comment about the black-skinned Malaysians. The racial comment certainly registered with Boston-Wright and she gladly accepted the Darlington's dinner invitation, hoping some more loose comments would flow during the night. Besides, her pantry was still particularly bare at home and this would save her buying a takeaway. Momentarily the thought of the Darlington's poisoning her did enter her mind but she quickly dismissed it.

"We appreciate you dropping our things off. The photo takes pride and place on the mantle and the little figurine was passed onto Kay by her mother," Darlington said.

"I could see they were personal. I just wanted to get them back to you sooner rather than later," Boston-Wright replied, putting on her best face of empathy as she gently stared into each of their eyes.

Darlington knocked back the last third of his glass of beer and suggested they move to the dining table for dinner. He took up the head of the table position, with Mrs. Darlington sitting to his right. The table sported a white lace tablecloth and Mrs. Darlington had decided to use their best silverware for the occasion. Even silver napkin rings with white cloth napkins sat beside each plate. Boston-Wright took up her seat opposite Kay and complimented her on her fine table, offering that it reminded her of special dinners with her family and that her mother always presented the table similarly. Mrs. Darlington appreciated the compliment by nodding and smiling.

Mick Darlington removed the lid to the silver urn, revealing a rich Beef Tikka Marsala curry, its aroma filling the room. Boston-Wright's eyes widened and hummed her pleasure at the best, most authentic looking curry she had seen in a long time. Darlington grabbed the ladle and served a generous scoop onto Boston-Wright's plate, asking if she would like more, his eyebrows raised and head slightly cocked as he spoke. Boston-Wright waved her hands indicating no as she grabbed the plate and moved toward the steamed rice. Mrs. Darlington held up a basket of freshly made roti bread, suggesting Boston-Wright should put one on her side plate.

Kay Darlington said grace before they started dinner. It had been a long time since she had heard grace at a table and was glad Mrs. Darlington didn't invite her to deliver the words. Finishing off with the customary Amen, Boston-Wright looked up at Mrs. Darlington, nodded and smiled. Mrs. Darlington definitely appeared the more conservative of the two, but she didn't pick her to be religious. Not that religious people have a particular look. Her Uncle Albert always said grace before his meal but swore like a trooper.

"So, Jo, are we still suspects in your investigation?" Darlington asked as he spooned some rice into his mouth.

Boston-Wright was a little taken aback. Darlington had fired a big gun early, perhaps to test the waters. She remembered Pratt saying that such killers like to feel in control and want to exude confidence. Boston-Wright needed to be tactical here. If she said no, then there may be no comeback in the future. If she said yes, and that was still the case, then the Darlington's would clam up and the rest of the dinner would be quiet and awkward.

"We are working through things, Mick. That's why I wanted to return your personal items. They are not needed in the case, and besides, I know how important they are to you both." Boston-Wright shifted her eyes to Kay as she spoke. Mrs. Darlington dropped her eyes to her meal, toying with her food with her fork. Mick seemed to accept her answer as he took another bite.

"Are you any closer to making an arrest?" Darlington asked.

"We have a few things we are working on," Boston-Wright replied as Darlington topped up her glass with beer.

"Like what?" Darlington enquired. "Or can't you say?" Boston-Wright knew she had to leak out a bit of information to keep the conversation flowing, hoping Darlington would slip up.

"Well, I'm not supposed to talk about cases outside the team. I could lose my job if this got out," Boston-Wright remarked as Darlington moved in his seat and leaned forward slightly.

"One common thing in all the murders is that the victims were handcuffed with Smith & Wesson cuffs. They are very rare. In fact, it's only the Army who use them in great quantity."

"Oh, so you think because I was in the Army, the Military Police, to be exact, that I would have these cuffs in my possession? We are decent people, Detective. Nothing kinky here," Darlington protested.

Boston-Wright realized that she had hit a nerve. Darlington was now sitting back in his chair, looking around the room with an annoyed look on his face. Boston-Wright needed to calm the situation and get things back on a friendly keel. Besides, Mrs. Darlington didn't look like the tying up type, more of a missionary style girl and only on special occasions, she thought.

"Oh no, Mick. You haven't been in the Army for a long time. I wouldn't assume you'd have any handcuffs," Boston-Wright replied in a soft, almost girlish voice. Darlington seemed to accept her reply and leaned forward, resting his elbows on the table, much to Mrs. Darlington's look of disgust.

"Sure, we used Smith & Wesson handcuffs when I was in the force. In fact, the boys gave me a few pairs when I retired. But we threw them out in a council curbside collection about three years ago, didn't we Kaysie?" Mrs. Darlington nodded and looked over at Jo.

"What took you to Sydney?" Darlington asked.

"Sydney?" Boston-Wright responded in a surprised tone. How did he know both she and Creed were in Sydney investigating the case?

"I rang the station to see if you had finished with our things and the desk chap said that you and that Creed fellow were in Sydney on a case," Darlington replied once again, seeking to show his superiority and that he was in control, something else Pratt mentioned was a trait with such serial killers.

"Oh, yes we were in Sydney following up some leads. But like I said, I can't really talk too much about it," Boston-Wright replied, finalizing with a long pause, her mouth gaping open. "What I can say is that we have noticed there have been similar murders down there in between the killings here in the Tweed." Boston-Wright stared at Darlington and then smiled. She gave both of them a few moments to jump back into the conversation, but both Mr. & Mrs. Darlington remained quiet.

"Dessert, love?" Mrs. Darlington asked, trying to change the subject and remove herself from the table. "It's only apple pie and ice cream."

"That would be lovely. It'll nicely finish off your wonderful curry," Boston-Wright complimented Mrs. Darlington as she handed her plate to her.

Mrs. Darlington returned with three generous portions of homemade apple pie. Boston-Wright twirled her plate around admiring the golden brown, crunchy crust and volumes of moist apples and cinnamon, just like her grandma used to bake. The pie was complimented with a decent scoop of Sara Lee French Vanilla ice cream; its creaminess helped the warm pie slide down with a cool tingle.

The mood had changed a little. Darlington seemed a little distant and less friendly. Boston-Wright sensed his coolness, so she tried to invigorate the conversation.

"This looks like a nice street," Boston-Wright commented as she savored another spoonful of pie.

"It has been. When we first came here about 20 years ago, it was very pleasant," Darlington replied.

"Nice and quiet," Mrs. Darlington threw in.

"The Thompsons moved in about, um, 13 or 14 years ago. Sam was just a little kid. Disadvantaged family but nice enough," Darlington added.

"But then he grew up," Mrs. Darlington said as she gathered the dessert plates, stacked them and was about to exit to the kitchen. "You can't help that kind. Welfare bludgers."

Darlington smiled at Boston-Wright as Mrs.

Darlington retreated to the kitchen. "Kaysie has no time for them. It's her North Queensland upbringing." Boston-Wright nodded, pushing her chair back from the table and announcing that she had to get home.

Darlington stood in unison and moved toward Boston-Wright, giving her a hug. "Thank you so much for dropping our things off. You don't know how much it means to us both. And thanks for staying for dinner. We enjoyed your company. We hope you still don't think we are suspects."

Boston-Wright thanked the Darlington's for a pleasant evening and made her way down the dimly lit driveway to her car, her heart pumping. With her hand shaking, she fumbled her keys as she hit the unlock button and hopped into her car. She never looked back up at the house but she felt the Darlington's were watching.

It was 9.20pm as Boston-Wright turned on the lights in her house, kicked off her shoes and made her way to her bedroom. She tossed her bag onto her bed and gave herself a quick look in the mirror, massaging her face at the same time.

The doorbell rang. Who could it be at this time of night? Surely Darlington didn't follow her home. Boston-Wright's heart raced as she neared the door.

"Who is it?" she called out.

"It's me. Open up."

"Sir, what the hell are you doing here at this hour?" Boston-Wright replied as she unlatched the door and opened it.

"I just let the surveillance boys go home, so I wanted to find out how it went," Creed replied as he barged his way in, tossing his keys onto the coffee table, unconcerned about scratching it. He plonked himself down on the sofa and asked if Boston-Wright was making coffee.

"No, sir, I'm not. I'm bushed, actually."

"Well, what did they say?"

"Not a lot. They seemed quite pleasant. Sort of reminded me a bit of my parents," Boston-Wright commented, her head dropped and her eyes filling with tears.

"Oh great. So you got bloody nothing," Creed snapped, insensitive to Boston-Wright's feelings. With that, he snatched his keys off the table and made his way to the door. "Good night. I need your report on my desk first thing," he said as he slammed the door and left.

Boston-Wright slumped back into her lounge. She felt hopeless and worthless. Why couldn't she do anything right?

CHAPTER 15

Boston-Wright typed feverishly away at her report, silently thanking for spell check. The words weren't flowing easily, her mind clouded by thoughts of her parents. Mick and Kay Darlington had in many ways reminded Boston-Wright of her parents, an elderly couple enjoying the quiet life and each other's company. But for Boston-Wright, she would never be able to share those moments any more with her parents. She just couldn't see how Mick Darlington was their murderer.

Creed called for Boston-Wright to join him and Pratt in the incident room. Boston-Wright handed over her report to both of them as she sat at the meeting table. Smith joined them with coffee from Jarrod's next door. Boston-Wright took a sip of her latte, thanked Smith for her thoughtfulness and savored the full bean taste of her double shot. Smith appreciated the compliment, which was more than could be said for the two chauvinists at the end of the table who seemed engrossed in Boston-Wright's report.

"So, I take it nothing much happened, Boston-Wright," Pratt concluded, tossing the report back onto the table. "Let's go through it step by step, shall we."

"I see Darlington immediately showed his superiority in the family by waiting at the door when you arrived. He was clearly demonstrating that he had nothing to hide by welcoming you into his home," Pratt started.

"I guess so but it could have easily been Mrs. Darlington who opened the door," Boston-Wright replied.

"Maybe, but not in the case of our Mr. Darlington. That was all pre-meditated," Pratt commented. Creed nodded, showing his acceptance of Pratt's analysis.

"You were invited for dinner. Once again Mick Darlington wanted to show you he had nothing to hide by keeping you in their home longer."

"Yes, that's true but it was only a curry, Pratt," Boston-Wright replied.

"And was there enough for their late, unexpected dinner guest? You only rang him at 6pm to say you were dropping his things off. Curries generally take a few hours to cook, don't they? It may have not been last night but Mick Darlington was waiting to invite you in at some stage. He's playing a game, Boston-Wright."

"He was genuinely pleased to get their things back," Boston-Wright stated.

"Yes. He was allowing you into his private world. You had something personal of theirs and he wanted to let you think you were special, possibly even one of the family," Pratt went on. Boston-Wright looked back at him with thoughts of her parents and the Darlington's inter-mixing in her mind.

"I see here you write that he asked you about Sydney," Pratt said, referring back to the report. "He said he phoned the station and was told that both you and Jack were in Sydney investigating more murders."

"Yes, he did throw me with that one," Boston-Wright replied, leaning back in her seat and running her hands through her hair.

"You know the drill, Boston-Wright. The front desk never would give out your whereabouts, let alone advise what you both were doing in Sydney."

"I'd have their balls if they did," Creed said gruffly.

"And, finally, he plays his trump card. He gives you a 'fatherly' hug and asks if he is still a suspect, all the while putting on his best paternal look. Am I right?" Pratt asks.

"Spot on, Detective" Boston-Wright sighed.

"He got you. And that's exactly what he wanted the whole night. To bring you into his world and develop a bond between both of you. Tell me, Boston-Wright, is he our man?" Pratt asked.

"I'm not sure, Detective Pratt."

"He's clever, Jack. The cocky shit now thinks he's got a friend inside the investigation. Mark my words, he'll call you again, Boston-Wright." Pratt finished sliding his report over to Creed, who sat there empty faced and wondering if he should have sent a more experienced officer to return the Darlington's things.

Smith sat through the entire discussion without uttering a word, not even a comforting glance to her fellow female comrade. She too thought that Boston-Wright would have stuffed up.

"And when he does, Boston-Wright, he'll want to help you with the investigation. Maybe even have a potential suspect for you," Pratt concluded as he pushed back on his chair, stood and walked out of the incident room. Creed gathered the notes into the file, looked at Boston-Wright with disappointment, and stood to leave the room.

"I'll do better next time, sir," Boston-Wright threw out, hoping to redeem herself with Creed. She glanced at Smith but didn't seek her approval.

"There won't be another time, Boston-Wright. You can fill your time in doing research here in the station," Creed replied, leaving the room, his shoulders sunken like a defeated boxer.

Boston-Wright clasped her mouth to hold in the squeal as she rushed to the lady's toilets, arriving just in time as the flood gate of tears burst down her face. With her hands resting on the basin, she looked into the mirror, mentally scolding herself that she'll never be as good as her late father.

Creed was summoned upstairs. He knew the call was coming and he knew a pasting from the Chief Super was coming. O'Halloran was right on cue. The case budget was exploding and still there was no arrest. Creed was criticized for sending an inexperienced officer into a suspect's home trying to gain vital information. The Divisional Chief was applying the pressure to scale back the operation and O'Halloran was floundering in trying to convince him otherwise.

****

Boston-Wright left quietly through the rear of the station and headed home early. The grilling had taken its toll and she just wanted time to herself. She made a coffee and slumped into the sofa, flicking the Bold and Beautiful on the television for some mind-numbing relief. There was a soft knock on her door.

Boston-Wright peered through the peep hole. It was Kay Darlington. Boston-Wright wondered what to do. Should she call Creed? Another firm knock came. There was no time to call. Boston-Wright opened the door.

"Mrs. Darlington. What brings you here?" Boston-Wright asked.

"Just passing on my way to visiting one of my bridge playing partners and I thought you might like the rest of the curry we had last night. You seemed to enjoy it," Mrs. Darlington replied with a warm smile, gesturing to be allowed in. Boston-Wright stepped away from the doorway and allowed her in, taking the pot of curry as she passed.

"Can I get you a cup of tea?" Boston-Wright asked.

"No, dear. Just a quick visit mainly to drop off the curry and to show you this," Mrs. Darlington replied, diving into her handbag. Boston-Wright peered over at Mrs. Darlington, now sitting on the sofa, as she fumbled in her bag, one that had seen its best years some time ago.

"I have a newspaper clipping of your father opening the PCYC in Cabarita Beach. I thought you might like to see it."

"WOW! He was much younger there," Boston-Wright replied while looking at the 1997 date showing in the top right hand corner of the paper. And so do the other officers. Is that–"

"Tebbitt, the mongrel," Mrs. Darlington jumped in. "Dirty copper from the Vice Squad. He gave my Mick a horrible time years ago before they shipped him off to Queensland." Boston-Wright looked at Mrs. Darlington. It was evident she had no time for Peter Tebbitt, mentally agreeing with her from her own personal experience.

"You see the guy second from the left with the handle bar moustache?" Mrs. Darlington asked.

"Yep." Boston-Wright nodded, taking a closer look.

"That's Nick Finch. He now owns that gay bar, The Bear Club. He might be worth a talk to. I hear he has a club in the Cross as well," Mrs. Darlington explained.

"Funny, he doesn't look the gay type," Boston-Wright remarked, handing the newspaper clipping back. "I'll check him out, though." Boston-Wright thanked Mrs. Darlington, which was confirmed by a warm smile only to be broken by another loud knock at the door, causing both women to jump to their feet.

"It's the boss. He can't see you here, Mrs. Darlington."

"What's wrong, dear? I'm only dropping off your curry dinner."

Boston-Wright unlatched the door as Creed brushed past her into the lounge room, only to be surprised to see Mrs. Darlington. Holding his breath, his cheeks glowing a fiery red, he waited until Mrs. Darlington was out of the house.

"What the fuck was she doing here, Boston-Wright?" Before she could reply, Creed fired off, "I came around here to see if you were all right and I find you entertaining the wife of our number one suspect. Jesus Christ, Boston-Wright. Why didn't you ring?"

"I didn't get a chance, sir."

"So, what did she want?"

"She dropped off the rest of last night's curry and she had a newspaper clipping Mick Darlington found of my Dad opening the PCYC."

"You see. What have we been telling you? They are playing you. Getting you all emotional about your Dad, pretending they are your friends. It's bullshit, Jo. No more private meetings with them, ok?"

"Yes, sir, but she did offer up a name for us to look into."

"Oh really? Isn't that what Pratts's psych friend said would happen?" Creed said, shaking his head. "So, who is it anyway?"

"Nick Finch. He's the owner of The Bear Club and has another club in the Cross in Sydney" Boston-Wright said, looking at Creed, trying to redeem herself. But he wasn't buying. He still had a disgusted look on his face, sighing as he went to the door to leave.

"I'll check him out. We spoke to a waiter there, Walsh, I think. Yeah, yeah, Walsh. As camp as a row of tents. I'm going to put your place under surveillance. I want to know if the Darlington's come back. I suggest you lock all your windows and doors, just to be on the safe side. Good night, Boston-Wright."

CHAPTER 16

Nick Finch had a rap sheet as long as your arm. Running an illegal brothel, living off the means derived from prostitution, assault and a stint in the Arthur Gorrie Correctional Center for manslaughter. He sounded like one mean bastard.

Pratt passed the rap sheet onto Creed, commenting that perhaps Darlington had done them a favour. Creed returned a non-convincing smile but agreed Finch should be investigated.

"Some good news, Jack. The Pottsville boys have Finch in custody. He gave a hooker a nasty slap around the chops last night, breaking her jaw. And just for the record, she is black," Pratt commented with his eyebrows raised.

The two detectives organized themselves for the forty-minute trip south to Pottsville. Pratt was on coffee duty and Creed fired off a few last-minute duties for the troops while they were away. He made a point of reminding Boston-Wright to remain in the office and to go over the files, just in case they had missed anything. Creed gave a look to Smith as if to say to keep an eye on Boston-Wright. She got the message and continued typing.

"Not on tour today?" Smith asked Boston-Wright. "He normally takes you. I thought you two were quite chummy."

"Not today, or tomorrow or possibly ever," Boston-Wright replied with a stern look on her face. "The sooner this case wraps up the better. I can't wait to get off it."

"Oh, sweetie, I thought you liked it here," Smith replied in a patronizing tone.

"He's just an arrogant, self-centered, egotistical, fucking prick," Boston-Wright stated forcibly, clinching her right hand into a fist. "I just want to punch the bastard."

"Hey, steady down, Princess. We all like him around here and I won't have you bad mouthing him behind his back." Smith returned fire. "Sure, he can be a bit over the top from time to time, but he's an old traditionalist. Something missing in younger men these days. Are you pissed off because he gave you a mouthful about letting Mrs. Darlington into your house?" Boston-Wright stopped gazing around and looked back sharply at Smith.

"Oh, so you heard. What is this? Everybody talking about my business behind my back?" Boston-Wright looked disgusted, frustrated and annoyed.

"Quite the contrary. He's got your back. He's taken you under his wing. He was just concerned that Darlington was weaving his way into your life and that you could end up in trouble."

"Well, I don't need a father figure," Boston-Wright snapped back.

"Stop being such a prima donna, Jo. Creed is just caring. He's like that with all of us. But let me tell you something for nothing. Don't get him off side. It'll be the worst career mistake you'll ever make." Smith finished up and returned to her typing. Boston-Wright grabbed her bag and walked next door to Jarrod's coffee shop for a change of scenery.

Creed and Pratt made good time to Pottsville in spite of stopping off at Cabarita Hill to gather some fresh air and to check out the day's surfing action. The breaks were full of surfers, a place both boys wished they were even though neither of them could stand on a board. The duty sergeant welcomed his colleagues from Kingscliff and showed them into his office.

"A bit of a savage bastard," the sergeant said, passing Finch's record over to Creed while Pratt read over his shoulder.

"We picked him up at about half eleven last night from a laneway next to the Bull & Keg. It took three bouncers to restrain him until we arrived."

"How old is this guy?" Pratt asked.

"Um, late forties. Yep, 48," the sergeant replied.

"We've had him in a few times before but nothing as brutal. He loves the grog but the boys thought he might have been on ice last night. He's a bit of a no hoper. He's got that gay bar up in Caba and a share in another in the Cross but he pisses his money up against the wall. Lives in a basement flat at the back of Cabarita Lakes owned by Kerry Douglas, an old hooker from way back."

"He seems to like the hookers," Creed said, looking over his convictions.

"Especially the dark ones. His mother was aboriginal and his old man was a sailor in the merchant navy. He pissed off when Nick was just a lad," the sergeant commented.

"Does he drive?" Creed asked.

"Sort of. He's got a beat up, clapped out Nissan Patrol. We've had it impounded for a week, outstanding parking and traffic fines.

Creed and Pratt were shown the interview room and waited for Finch to be brought in. They didn't have to wait long. They could hear footsteps and some drunk trying to sing a Joe Cocker ballad.

Fife was shown to the other side of the interview table. He was smaller than Creed expected, although his part aboriginal heritage was evident. His black, slicked back hair looked like a leftover from the eighties and badly in need of a shampoo. His Hawaiian shirt had grass stains and the right sleeve showed a splashing of blood, assumed from wiping his busted nose. His dossier also highlighted that he was a former Golden Gloves champ when he was sixteen.

"What's this all about?" Finch asked, standing behind his chair.

"I'm Detective Sergeant Jack Creed and this is Detective Greg Pratt. We'd like to ask you a few questions about a case we are working on."

"Are you having a fuckin' lend of me? Creed and Pratt. Are you auditioning for the remake of Starsky and Hutch?" Finch sarcastically replied with a big grin. The two detectives looked at each other and thought how they'd both like to wipe the smirk off Finch's face.

"We are investigating a series of murders. We would like to eliminate you from our enquiries," Pratt said, gritting his teeth.

"I want a solicitor before I speak to you two bozos. You're not going to fit me up with any murders," Finch said, also demanding a cigarette and coffee. Creed slid over a packet of Marlborough heavies and a $2 Bic lighter. The constable left the room to find a duty solicitor from the station's panel. Creed and Pratt also exited the room to grab another coffee and a couple of Arnott's biscuits from the staff kitchen.

The Kingscliff detectives were expecting a podgy, old suburban solicitor to show up for Finch, considering the limited choice one would expect in Pottsville. Casey Edwards, 20-something, blond in a well-cut charcoal grey suit over a soft pink French cuffed shirt, was nothing like they expected. Finch also pepped up and straightened his shirt at the sight of Ms. Edwards.

Creed threw down a photo of Jessica Campbell, the hooker from Pottsville who was brutally murdered. Finch picked up the photo, held it close, squinting as he ran his eyes over the victim and finally nodded that he knew the girl. As he began to speak, Edwards cautioned him to think before he spoke.

"It's okay, love. I've got nothing to hide. Yes, I knew her, if you know what I mean," Finch replied, looking at Creed. "She was special. If I had a win at the pokies, I'd give Jess a call. I was sorry to hear she got killed."

Creed placed down two more photos – Tom Langley and Darlene Ferguson.

"Yep, he was her pimp," Finch recalled, drawing on his cigarette. "Old Tommy was a fuckin' rogue. She was half his age. I think she thought of him as a father figure but that old prick had her on the game. She used to do half the blokes in the caravan park where she worked while their wives were out shopping."

"Really?" chimed in Pratt.

"Mate, it was well-known. I think the park manager must have been in on it. There was never a vacancy at the Hastings Point Caravan Park." Finch coughed and spluttered on his cigarette.

Creed looked at Pratt. It was time to play their trump card. Creed placed down Mick Darlington's photo and pushed it closer to Finch.

"Do you know this guy?" Creed asked.

"Sure. I bought a car off him. Well, his wife anyway," Finch replied.

"And what car was that?" Pratt asked.

"The old Nissan Patrol these buggers have got locked up just because of a few parking fines," Finch stated, looking over at the duty sergeant. Creed couldn't believe his ears. The Darlington's had told him the car had been stolen by some aboriginal kids.

"We had it down as being stolen," Creed commented.

"Yeah, it kind of was. A couple of the local lads stole it, took it for a joy ride and trashed it inside. But the coppers found it and returned it to the Darlington's, who were keen to get rid of it. So, Mick and I got chatting and I decided to buy it. The back seat was carved up and had a big stain on it. I called Col Turner from Turner's Wreckers and he fitted me a new one."

"What did Mr. Turner do with the old back seat?" Pratt asked.

"Probably burnt it. It was cactus. He couldn't have sold it."

"You mentioned Mick Darlington and you spoke about buying the car. Did you already know him?" Creed asked.

"Yeah, we were in the Army together. The Military Police, actually. We never socialized once we got out. I don't think Mrs. Darlington approved of me. But I used to see them around a bit," Finch recalled, looking into Creed's cigarette packet while holding up his empty coffee mug, indicating to the constable to get him another. "Hold the lobster roll," Finch chuffed as the constable left the interview room.

"So you would see Mick Darlington around. Anywhere in particular?" Pratt asked.

"Well, he is a handyman with that old bugger's organization. Dad's something or another, and down at the Hastings Point Van Park. Let's just say that's one of his favorite haunts and that Mrs. Darlington would do a lot of shopping offsite." Finch smirked, giving Creed a wink.

"Well, Mr. Finch, you've been most helpful. I think this establishment will be enjoying your company for another night, so we may pop back tomorrow to ask you a few more questions. Ms. Edwards." Creed stood and moved to the door of the interview room.

"Hope you'll put a good word in for me, Detective."

Creed turned, half smiled and both he and Pratt left the station. It was ten to six and Creed invited his fellow officer to stop off at the Beach Hotel in Cabarita Beach to have a drink and an early dinner. The chicken parmigiana was right up Pratt's street and Creed couldn't pass up a 400g rump, well done, over a flame grill fire.

"We'll get the boys over to Finch's place in the morning to check out his flat and forensics to give his Patrol a thorough going over in the Pottsville Police Station carpark," Creed said as he clinked Pratt's glass, followed by the customary 'cheers.'

"Do you still think Mick Darlington is our man, Jack?"

"Not sure. Finch is certainly in the frame. Let's see what the boys turn up in the morning. I might be wrong on our Mr. Darlington after all."

"Let's not let Boston-Wright into that little confession just yet," Pratt said with a smirk.

"Right on, Greg. Your shout." Creed smiled as he sunk back into his chair and looked through the restaurant, over the sand dunes and onto the beach. The waves crashed onto the shore in a steady rhythm.

CHAPTER 17

Finch's flat was an absolute pig's squalor. It was evident the upstairs landlady never ventured inside. Creed had organized forensics and a couple of constables to give the place a thorough going over, not wanting to dirty his own hands, of course.

The team entered the property via the glass slider, the handle sticky with dirt and grime. Luckily everybody wore gloves, though the thought of organizing a tetanus shot for everybody had crossed their minds. The entrance to the front door was littered with cigarette butts with ash caked into the running track of the door.

The carpet, ala 1975, was well- worn, stained and had a distinctive odor of stale beer. It was evident Mr. Finch never owned a vacuum cleaner either. The furnishings weren't much better. A two seater card table sat next to the kitchenette; neither chairs matching. The team moved into Finch's bedroom, which was small to say the least. The Queen ensemble was perched under a window covered with a floral print curtain, definitely in need of a wash. The bed was unmade; its white sheets grey in color.

The usual stash of Playboy magazines, a half empty cup of coffee and a dirty ashtray sat beside the bed. The chest of drawers contained a modest range of underwear, socks and attire but at the back of the top drawer Constable Peters came across a bag of tablets, assumed to be ecstasy, with an estimated street value of $20,000.

Rummaging through the clothes closet was even more fruitful. A hessian shoulder bag bearing the initials D F inside was stuffed in behind some old shoe boxes. Could this belong to Darlene Ferguson? While the forensic team bagged up the evidence, Constable Peters telephoned Creed, who was having breakfast with Pratt at the Blue Rose café in Cabarita Beach.

"We've come across a bag of E, sir, and a hessian shoulder bag with the initials D F inside the flap. Forensics are bagging it up now." Creed complimented the constable for his good work and motioned to Pratt to finish up his coffee so they could continue onto Pottsville.

"The boys have found some dope and a bag that might be Darlene Ferguson's," Creed crowed. "We'll be able to keep our Mr. Finch in custody for a little longer yet."

****

While the second forensic team was stripping Finch's Patrol apart at the Pottsville Station, Boston-Wright had headed off to Turner's Wreckers to follow up on the stained, torn seat he replaced.

"How can I help you, love?" Colin Turner asked Boston-Wright as she carefully tiptoed her way through the mud leading into the yard. Dozers moved rapidly in a zigzag fashion across the lot, moving body parts from one point to another. The noise was deafening.

"Yes, I'm Detective Constable Jo Boston-Wright," she said, showing her badge. I believe you sold a rear bench seat for a late nineties Nissan Patrol to a Mr. Nick Finch earlier this year," Boston-Wright stated.

"Come into the office, love. I'll need to check my paperwork."

The office was as messy as the yard. A port-a-com shed raised on concrete Besser blocks was the headquarters for this enterprise. Turner's desk was covered in files, receipts, a half empty can of Coke, and a partially eaten bacon and egg roll. Mr. Turner invited Boston-Wright to have a seat but looking at the thick coating of dust, she declined, preferring to preserve her new suit by standing. A girly calendar from Mick's Spanners donned the wall. Boston-Wright tugged her lapels closer after looking at Miss May.

"Here we go," Turner commented as he found the paperwork for the sale, showing Boston-Wright.

"Why did he need it replaced?" Boston-Wright asked.

"Um, it was pretty buggered. Some kids I believe had stolen the car and trashed it. Slashed the seat and it had a dark red stain on the right side. The seat was unrepairable."

"A red stain?" Boston-Wright asked.

"Yeah, it was caked in. Probably been there for a while. Most likely one of the little shits rubbed some tomato sauce or beetroot on it," Turner recalled shrugging his shoulders.

"Do you still have the seat?" Boston-Wright enquired, looking out into the yard. A bead of perspiration trickled down her back as she motioned toward the office door.

"Nah. It was crap. We burnt it. Nothing to be salvaged there."

Boston-Wright thanked Mr. Turner for his time and walked gingerly back to her car, wiping the excess mud off her shoes on the footpath grass before she got in. She telephoned Creed and passed on her findings, asking if he wanted her to come to Pottsville. He declined. Boston-Wright drove back to the Kingscliff Station feeling her position on the team was still shaky. One little slipup and she was right back to square one. She couldn't believe Creed was that unforgiving.

****

Yesterday, Creed and Pratt acted out the good cop, good cop routine with Finch. They needed information from him, but today's interview would have a totally different tone. Finch was already seated in the interview room, chain smoking as usual. The detectives sat opposite, placing the items found in his flat on the floor.

"Looks like you might be spending a bit more time as a guest of Her Majesty's service," Creed started off, producing the bag of ecstasy onto the table. Finch's head jerked backwards; a stunned look engrossed his face.

"Never seen that stuff ever in my life," Finch protested, drawing heavily on his cigarette.

"Well, we'll let the fingerprint boys determine that for us," Pratt commented. Finch rubbed his chin; his look now more worried than stunned. But things were about to get a whole lot worse.

"The courts can ultimately sort out your stay with that stuff. I'm more interested in this bag," Creed stated, leaning down onto the floor and producing the hessian shoulder bag, neatly placing it on the interview table and positioning it so the initials D F were clearly visible to Finch. Finch began to visibly shake, grasping for the cigarette packet to light up another smoke.

"We believe this bag was owned by Darlene Ferguson," Creed stated. Pratt glanced at Creed, knowing full well that hadn't been determined by forensics yet. "How come it was stuffed down the back of your wardrobe?"

Fife sat back in his chair for a moment. The silence was deafening. He knew he was cornered.

"Ok, if I tell you, can we cut a deal with the ecstasy sting?" Finch asked.

"No deals, Mr. Finch, but I am happy to put in a good word to the judge that you co-operated with us. That's providing you tell us the truth, of course," Creed replied.

"Darlene and her pimp Tom did a bit of moonlighting for me at the clubs in the area. The kids would go nuts for the stuff and Darlene was a pretty good salesperson. Anyway, the day she turned up dead, I found her bag discarded amongst some trees at the back of the van park. She had a bit of my stuff inside left over from the weekend, so I chucked the bag in the car and took it home. Last thing I needed back then was for the coppers to find the bag, my dope and a wad of cash from the weekend sales and link me into the case."

"So, had you arranged to meet Darlene that day to get your money?" Pratt asked.

"Much later. Seven that night. No, I was driving past on my way to Pottsville when I saw all the cop cars and the blue tape up everywhere. So, I stopped in and the manager told me. I nearly shit myself. I needed a piss, so I used the toilets down the back of the park and that's when I found the bag. I saw the strap protruding from the grass between the trees. I felt relieved, but it was a horrible thing that had happened to little Darlene."

Creed wasn't 100% convinced about Finch's story; the man was a pathological liar. However, for the moment, until forensics could confirm it was Darlene's bag, they could at least hang onto Mr. Finch for a while longer. Creed ordered the attending constable to charge Finch with possession of ecstasy while he and Pratt left the station for the drive back to Kingscliff.

"What do you make of all that, Jack? Is Finch still in the frame?" Pratt asked.

"Not sure. Let's get a press release out saying we have a man in custody for drug possession and we are continuing our investigation into the recent spate of murders. Run it by O'Halloran first, though."

Creed walked straight into his office, oblivious of who was still at the station. Pratt made a smart-arse comment to Smith that Boston-Wright must have had an early night. Smith gave a half smile and raised her right eyebrow and then continued on typing.

Pratt grabbed two cold beers from the kitchen and walked into Creed's office, lifting the pull tag as he plonked a can in front of Creed. It was after five and a cold beer would go down well.

"O'Halloran okayed the press release," Pratt said, taking a sip of his beer.

"Well, this will liven things up a bit," Creed replied, his feet resting on the corner of his desk.

"I'm sure Finch won't be reading the morning paper, Jack." Pratt thought for a minute. "Don't tell me you still think Darlington is in the frame?"

"Never out of it, Pratty. Tell me this. Why does a guy, suddenly remember a fellow serving officer and put him in the frame for murder just as we were turning up the heat on him?" Creed asked while gesturing with his hands open.

"No, our Mr. Darlington is still very much a person of interest," Creed said, knocking back his beer and thumping the empty can down on the table. An air of confidence had returned to Jack Creed.

"We are getting close, Pratty. Very close."

CHAPTER 18

The next morning Finch was marched screaming into the Kingscliff Magistrates Court, charged with possession of an illegal drug. Creed and the team also wanted to pin the Ferguson murder on him but their evidence was light. Finch would be kept in custody for a while longer before the Magistrate passed sentencing for his drug conviction, which hopefully was enough time for Creed to cement his case.

Creed called a quick meeting with the team, advising them of the conviction for Finch on drug charges. Boston-Wright was publicly congratulated for her hard work on the case, although she didn't fully accept it. Creed had given her enough bollockings over the past few weeks that she was close to quitting. However, it was nice to hear something positive from Creed. Creed retired to his office, calling Boston-Wright in and motioning for her to close the door.

"I meant what I said out there. You have contributed well to the team. I can be a cranky old bastard at times but I usually have people's best interests in mind," Creed said his voice adding weight.

"Thank you, sir. I do appreciate it," Boston-Wright replied.

"Now one other thing; we did get a trace on your prank call. It came from Darlington's place."

"Hmm, so Mrs. Darlington turning up with a newspaper article was no coincidence then," Boston-Wright remarked.

"No. It appears not. I've decided to put a permanent tap on your home phone until this whole thing is cleaned up. I suggest you don't answer unidentified calls from your mobile at night. I'm also going to have the boys do hourly drive-bys at night as well. We can't be too careful."

"What about the budget, sir?"

"Fuck the budget, Boston-Wright. We have a police officer's life possibly in jeopardy and no officer is getting killed on my watch. O'Halloran can shove that in his pipe and smoke it," Creed let off with gusto. Boston-Wright appreciated Creed's concern. Maybe she was making inroads after all.

The van from Nerang Correctional arrived at around 2pm and Finch was brought into the interview room via the rear of the station. He looked remarkably well, although the orange prison overalls weren't flattering. A good night sleep, a clean shave and a meal seemed to have done wonders for him.

Creed and Boston-Wright entered the interview room, sitting down opposite Finch, who was still restrained with handcuffs. As Creed introduced Boston-Wright to Finch and his new legal aid solicitor, since the last couldn't handle the case any further, Creed ordered the constable to remove Finch's handcuffs. Finch shook his wrists, rubbing them to get the blood flowing more freely and showed his appreciation by nodding to Creed.

"Where's your other cranky mate? This one is a lot better on the eye though," Finch commented, giving Boston-Wright his best smile, although his missing side tooth didn't make it flawless. Boston-Wright wondered to herself how losers seem to gravitate toward her. She took a deep breath, looked down and then to Creed to start the interview.

Creed referred back to his notes from the day earlier, getting Finch to go over the same story just in case some vital points aired themselves from Finch's loose flowing lips.

"One thing that did stick in my mind was Mrs. Darlington," Finch recalled, drawing on his cigarette.

"How so?" Boston-Wright asked.

"She looked like she had just seen a ghost. She was as white as a sheet when the coppers cordoned the place off."

"I suppose she was horrified by the news of Ms. Ferguson's death," Boston-Wright added. "Where was Mr. Darlington? Wasn't he comforting her?" Boston-Wright asked.

"No, I saw the old prick at Woolworths in Cabarita Beach about 15 minutes earlier," Finch replied, breaking out into a sweat and lightly puffing and blowing. Creed asked if he was okay.

"Just the booze, brother. Haven't had a drink for a couple of days. Really need one about now," Finch commented, his hands starting to shake.

Creed wound up the interview, deciding it would be best to send Finch back to Nerang. No new startling evidence had come forward from their chat.

"Strange Mr. Darlington wasn't around, Jack, but Finch just happened to turn up when the body was found," Boston-Wright commented to Creed.

"Not really. Darlene Ferguson had been dead for over five hours before her body was found. Mick Darlington is still in my frame," Creed responded as he walked back into his office, wondering what tonight was going to bring.

As Jo said her goodbyes to the team, Pratt walked in and gave his update to Creed. Darlington had spent most of the day home except for a mid-morning walk to the newsagent to grab the daily paper. Mrs. Darlington was seen hanging out her washing at around 1.30pm. Creed reminded Pratt to ensure the patrol boys passed Jo's house regularly.

"Who's on tonight?" Creed asked.

"Thomas and Benson," Pratt replied, looking at the roster. "Good lads," he said, giving Creed an assuring nod.

****

Boston-Wright called into the supermarket to grab some essentials for an easy-to-cook dinner. Jamie Oliver's butterfly chicken breast in lemon and thyme seemed right up her alley; 45 minutes in the oven and a garden salad and dinner would be served.

As Boston-Wright packed her groceries into the boot of her car, her mobile rang. She pressed the green button, cocked the phone between her chin and shoulder, and placed the bags carefully in the boot, tying the handles so the groceries wouldn't spill.

"Hello," Boston-Wright said with a sigh as she lifted the heavy bags off the car park floor into her car. There was no answer. She released the grocery bags and viewed her phone. It read, 'No Caller ID.'

"Hello? Hello?" she repeated in a louder tone.

"Oh, Detective Boston-Wright, it's me," the old male voice responded. Boston-Wright knew exactly who this was, but how did he get her mobile phone number?

"Mr. Darlington, why are you calling me?" Boston-Wright asked, her heart racing a million miles an hour. She rubbed her chest, trying to calm herself.

"I just thought I'd see how your case was coming along?" Darlington asked.

"Mr. Darlington, you know I can't discuss a case I'm working on."

"Oh, it's okay to question me, but you're not willing to share anything back?" Darlington fired in an annoyed, almost boyish tone. "The papers say you've arrested somebody?"

"Yes, that's right, but I can't discuss it any further," Boston-Wright replied.

"Is it that Finch chap I told you about?" Darlington enquired.

"Yes, but that's all I can say. I must go," Boston-Wright said.

"Okay, Detective Boston-Wright. Woolworths can be a busy place at night," Darlington said as he hung up.

Boston-Wright hit the hang up button on her mobile as she nervously looked around, scrolling through her contacts for the Kingscliff Station number. How did he know she was at Woolworths? Lucky guess? She could have been at Aldi.

Pratt answered the phone at the station. Boston-Wright asked for Creed without the obligatory hello. He could tell it was serious.

"He's gone home. Try his mobile. Everything okay?"

"Darlington just phoned me on my mobile. It's freaked me out. How did he get my number? I need to get hold of Creed," Boston-Wright said with a shaky voice.

"Stay put. I'll call his mobile. Just stay calm. I'll call you back," Pratt replied, trying to give Boston-

Wright some assurance that everything would be okay, although his voice didn't actually reek of confidence.

Greg Pratt momentarily became Boston-Wright's father figure and feverishly rang for Creed without luck. Creed always picked up; why not tonight? Not sure what to do, he telephoned Boston-Wright and gave her Creed's address.

"Get yourself over to Creed's place and let him know what's going on. I'll contact the patrol boys to be extra diligent tonight.

****

Boston-Wright pressed the buzzer for Unit 1 at the Seaview Motel. It was a modest establishment with great views over Cabarita Beach to the ocean. She unwittingly left her finger on the button longer than normal. The security door clicked open and Boston-Wright climbed the stairs to the first-floor apartment. The door was slightly ajar as Boston-Wright knocked and walked in, hoping not to be confronted by any surprises of Creed in a bath towel.

A young 20-something blond girl wearing just a bathrobe, her hair tied up into a bun with a towel greeted her and showed her through the kitchen onto the balcony. The apartment was tiny, magazines tossed on the coffee table and dishes stacked in the sink.

The young girl called out to Creed. "You have a visitor," she shouted toward the closed bedroom. Boston-Wright didn't know where to look. She felt awkward walking in on Creed's private life. Boston-Wright smiled at the girl, finding it hard to believe Jack could be so unfaithful to his wife, although she could understand if he was.

"Who is it?" Creed's booming voice came through the bedroom door.

"What's your name?" the young girl asked.

"Jo Boston-Wright," she replied, still having difficulties coming to grips with what she had just walked in on.

The bedroom door flung open, almost coming off its hinges. "Boston-Wright! What are you doing here?" Creed bellowed. Before she could answer, the young girl spoke.

"Dad, that's not a nice way to speak to a work colleague," and with that Melissa walked back through the apartment to the bathroom to dry her hair.

Creed nodded his head and sat down at the outdoor

setting. His bathrobe was frayed on the lapels and could do with a good soaking in Oxyfresh. His white slides weren't much better, obviously stolen from a 5-star hotel a long time ago. The 'S' insignia was a dead giveaway.

"Darlington phoned me while I was shopping at Woolies," Boston-Wright explained. "It freaked me out. I thought he must have been watching me."

"What did he want?" Creed asked with his business head on, not showing one ounce of interest in how Boston-Wright was feeling. She was clearly rattled.

Boston-Wright explained that Darlington was basically after an update. She reiterated that Pratt had mentioned this was something serial killers did; they wanted to revel in every detail of a case.

"We've got him rattled," Creed chimed in. "Go home but don't answer your mobile. He knows you will be home. He'll ring you. Make him do it on the house phone. We have it tapped."

Boston-Wright checked that every window was locked, then doubled checked just to be sure. This had been her home since she was a child. It was the one place where she felt safe, but not anymore. Every creak or rattle unnerved her. She had the place lit up like a Christmas tree.

Boston-Wright paced around like a cat on the hunt. Her appetite for dinner was completely gone; adrenalin was fueling her now. Her mobile rang. She almost jumped out of her skin. It had been set to receive nine rings before going to voicemail. They seemed to take forever. She stood over the phone on the kitchen benchtop looking at the screen. There was no caller ID showing. It must be Darlington. Even telemarketers don't work this late.

The mobile rang another three times. Boston-Wright gripped her top, looking at the screen and hoping it would stop. She was being driven to the point that she just wanted to pick it up. Her left hand hovered over the phone and then it stopped ringing. Boston-Wright felt immediate relief but still was none the wiser as to who had been ringing.

The house phone rang. She took a deep breath. After her third breath, she picked up the receiver.

"Hello?" she asked timidly.

"Hi, Jo, it's just Mick Darlington again. Don't you answer your mobile at night?" he asked.

"It's been playing up, Mr. Darlington. Something's wrong with the battery. How can I help you?" Boston-Wright asked.

"Have you eaten?" Darlington enquired.

"Yes, just had something light," Boston-Wright replied.

"Kay's made up a great beef stroganoff. Thought I might drop it off," Darlington said.

"No, that's okay. I'm sure it's great. Perhaps another time."

"It'll be better than that slop Finch will be eating tonight," Darlington went on.

"I guess so but I'm really tired and need an early night, Mr. Darlington."

"Did you charge him with the murders yet?"

"We are looking into it. We got him on the drug charges," Boston-Wright responded, hesitating to carry on. "You know I can't discuss the case, Mr. Darlington."

"Oh, come on, Detective. Finch is as guilty as sin," Darlington bounced back, a tone of annoyance entering his voice.

"He's pretty smart. He's hired himself a top-notch lawyer from Sydney."

"Smart? Finch? He's as dumb as dog shit," Darlington said, raising his voice. "My Kay can't stand him either. Says he's a creep. Undresses you with his eyes, she says."

There was a knock at the door. Boston-Wright felt relief that she had company but not wanting Darlington to go either so the call could be recorded longer, she invited him to stay on the line while she answered the door.

"Coming," Boston-Wright screamed out as she approached the door. Even though her heartbeat was still pounding in her chest from her call, she put on her best Oscar winning smile as she opened it.

"Evening, Jo," the guest said, pushing past her as he entered the lounge.

"Mr. Darlington, what are you doing here?" Boston-Wright said with astonishment, thinking it was one of her fellow officers who had been knocking.

"I brought you the beef stroganoff," he said as he placed the warm container on a chopping board on the kitchen bench.

Boston-Wright unlatched the deadlock and closed the front door. She quickly scampered down the hallway to the kitchen, not wanting Darlington to get out of sight. Mick Darlington noticing the receiver was off the hook on the benchtop, replaced it back in its cradle and thereby cutting Pratt off from listening in on the conversation.

Pratt immediately telephoned Creed, telling him that Darlington was inside Boston-Wright's house. Thomas had apparently stuffed up and missed Darlington leaving. The surveillance team was at least forty minutes away as they had been called to a pub brawl between two rival bikie gangs in Byron Bay. Creed, wearing just his tracky daks and a t-shirt, descended from his flat two steps at a time and quickly hightailed it to Boston-Wright's place.

Boston-Wright was uncomfortable. Her heart was almost bursting through her chest, her hands clammy and wet. She noticed Darlington had replaced the phone receiver; her lifeline to the outside world was now cut. She was hoping the surveillance team would come by soon and notice Darlington's car, but little did she know that wasn't going to happen.

"We couldn't have you not eating well, especially since you've solved the case," Darlington said, his voice cold and creepy.

"Thank you, Mr. Darlington, but you can't stay," Boston-Wright responded.

"I'll only stay for a minute. Aren't you going to offer me a coffee after my drive down here?"

"Mr. Darlington, you really must leave," Boston-Wright said, raising her voice as she walked backwards into the kitchen, the knife block just in vision from her right eye.

The front door swung open, its back hitting the umbrella stand, almost knocking it over.

"Jo, it's Jack," Creed said as he strode down the hallway to the kitchen. The relief on Jo's face was priceless.

"Mr. Darlington, what are you doing here?" Creed demanded, cutting him a stern look.

"Just dropped off a stew for Detective Boston-Wright. It's getting late. I must be off." Darlington brushed past Creed on his way to the front door. The sound of the Toyota Land Cruiser leaving her property calmed Boston-Wright's nerves and immediately brought some color back to her cheeks.

"What the fuck are you doing, Boston-Wright? You allowed Darlington into your house. Are you completely nuts?" Creed barked. "Put the kettle on and grab me a pillow and blanket. I'm sleeping here on the sofa tonight."

Boston-Wright stormed down the hallway to the linen closet and retrieved a spare blanket and pillow. She was seething under her breath that once again Creed hadn't asked her how she was but rather highlighted the mistakes she had made. Her grip on the pillow tightened as she entered the lounge visualizing it was Creed's head she was crushing.

Boston-Wright tossed the pillow and blanket at Creed and headed to her bedroom, closing the door with a spiteful, "Good night." But she was glad he was in the house.

CHAPTER 19

Boston-Wright thought having Creed sleeping on the sofa would calm her nerves and deliver her a peaceful night's sleep. Nothing could be further from the truth. It was a warm night and with the windows locked tight, the room was stifling. The ceiling fan offered some relief but its creaking, swirling noise made it more of a hindrance than a blessing.

The sheets on the bed looked as though they had been in a thrashing machine. Boston-Wright tossed from side to side, her head bursting with thoughts as she replayed the conversation with Darlington over and over again. At 2.30am Boston-Wright had given up the fight. She had been awake more often than asleep and sat up in bed, turning her bedside lamp on.

She grabbed a notebook and started to write out the conversation. Perspiration beaded on her forehead as she looked at the window, tempted to open it, but thought the better of it. The sound of the toilet flushing distracted her from her writing, dropping her eyes down to the underside of her bedroom door. A shadow passed by, indicating Creed returning to the sofa.

The clock radio alarm rang out at 6am, waking Boston-Wright from a deep sleep. She woke startled and groggy, her eyes feeling like she was covered in the thick blanket of cloud. The sound of pots and pans clanging hastened Jo out of her bedroom to the kitchen.

Jack was fossicking around under the kitchen sink looking for a fry pan to cook some bacon and eggs.

"Thought I might surprise you with some bacon and eggs," Creed explained with a smile. Jo stood before him, her hair a total mess. Her Tweetie bird pajamas were not flattering either.

"Sorry, Jack. No bacon or eggs. But there is Bircher muesli, Greek yoghurt and fresh strawberries if you are hungry."

"Not that bloody hungry. I'll grab something at McDonalds on the way home. Get cleaned up and I'll see you in the office by 8am."

"Okay, will do. And Jack? Thanks for last night,"

Boston-Wright said, knowing full well that Creed may have saved her life.

****

Creed called the team into the incident room. Pratt had called on his psychologist mate Dan Mitchell to sit on the playing of last night's recording of Boston-Wright and Darlington to give his expert account of the event. Boston-Wright felt a bit more under scrutiny but welcomed the analysis. This case was heating up and they needed to be on their game.

Mitchell highlighted Darlington's audacity to just show up. To him it indicated an air of confidence, a man wanting to show he was in control. Darlington's annoyance at Boston-Wright referring to Finch as being smart clearly brought out his frustration, as it seemed the focus was moving onto somebody else. Serial killers liked to be thought of as the smart one.

In Mitchell's eyes, Darlington was clearly using Boston-Wright to form a relationship. He was using her to get information on the case while at the same time trying to steer it in a particular direction by offering up certain information, like naming Finch as a potential suspect.

Boston-Wright didn't feel too good about being front and center in this discussion. She objected a few times to protest her vulnerability in that she was in control at all times. The other team members looked back with blank stares. They weren't buying it and Boston-Wright could see they weren't listening to her.

"Was I in any danger last night?" Boston-Wright asked, glancing around at the team as she directed her question to Mitchell.

"No, not last night. At the moment you are useful to him but that could change at any time," Mitchell remarked with a questioning, somewhat puzzled look on his face.

"But you don't seem convinced," Boston-Wright replied.

"Hm, it's not that necessarily. What puzzles me is that he didn't talk about the shoulder bag you found in Finch's flat. It would be the type of evidence that would further incriminate Finch."

"Maybe he didn't know it was found during our search," Boston-Wright said.

"Remember, Darlington gets off on being intelligent. He knew full well that you'd find drugs and the bag at Finch's place when you searched it.

No, just not normal for these types of killers to let something like that slide. They are calculating and Darlington would want to bury Finch fast. It's just odd," Mitchell explained.

"But he is our man?" Creed asked, to which Mitchell gave a questioning shrug.

"I don't have all the facts, Detective. That's where you come in," Mitchell replied.

Creed thanked Mitchell for his time and abandoned the meeting. In his mind Mick Darlington was still in the frame for all the murders; he just needed to figure out how he set up Finch. Creed jumped into Pratt's car, which had been idling in the carpark, to head back to Pottsville to question Finch. Boston-Wright stayed at Kingscliff to tidy up some loose ends.

The two detectives pulled into Pottsville Station just as Finch was being taken by the constable from the security van. He looked a little worse for wear with some cuts and bruises about the face. Pratt passed comment to Creed that Finch must not be making too many friends at Nerang.

"We have you for drug possession," Creed started, "but we want to talk to you more about Darlene Ferguson's murder."

"Like I keep on telling you, I didn't murder

anyone," Finch replied forcibly through a split lower lip.

"So you say but the evidence is against you," Pratt replied. Finch dropped his head and inhaled on his cigarette.

"You told us you knew Mick Darlington from the Army. When was the last time you saw him?" Creed asked.

"Like I said, at Woolies the day they found Darlene's body. Don't you listen?" Finch smarted.

"Listen here, Sunshine. You're in the hole for murder. You'll be spending 15 to 20 for this, and if we connect you to the other four murders, you'll get life. And considering how you look today, that won't be very pleasant for you, so I suggest you start paying attention," Creed warned.

"Has anybody come back into your life over the past few months? Any old business acquaintances, girlfriends, anybody?" Creed asked.

"Nope, not really. Except for some sheila who came to the club," Finch said, scratching his head.

"And who was she?" Pratt asked.

"Don't know. Walsh, my dish pig and doorman, came in and said there was a woman at the door asking after me. I thought she might be an old root or worse still I had got her up the duff and we had a kid and she was chasing money," Finch said.

"An old root?"

"Walsh said she was no spring chicken, so I immediately thought alimony. But by the time I got to the door, she had bolted."

The duty constable entered the room and slipped a note across to Creed, who stood and excused himself from the room. Boston-Wright was on the phone and needed to speak to him urgently.

"Jack, forensics have just phoned. They have found a piece of bubble gum wedged up under the passenger seat in Finch's car," Boston-Wright stated.

"Do they know what type?" Creed asked.

"Dubble Bubble," Creed replied.

"Never heard of it."

"And you most likely wouldn't have. It's American. We are seeing if there is a DNA match with Sharon Berg. And you know something else?" Boston-Wright commented. "It's around eight months old."

"Fife didn't own the car then. Darlington is our man! Good work, Boston-Wright. We're on our way back. See if you can get a DNA match."

Creed returned to the interview room with a grin from ear to ear. Finch looked up and feared the worse. Pratt wondered what the good news was that had changed Creed to such an upbeat look.

"Mr. Finch, you'll only be charged for drug possession. We've found our murderer."

CHAPTER 20

The big day had arrived. It was 6.30am at Kingscliff Police Station. The entire team had been assembled since six, all eager to finally bring this case to a close. Creed paced around his office like a kid on speech night. He reviewed the warrant over and over again. There could be no mistakes.

Pratt was in the carpark organizing two other patrol cars. This would be his last arrest; he wanted it to stick. Creed and Boston-Wright soon joined him, Jo opting for the back seat. You could cut the atmosphere with a knife. Pratt occasionally glanced at Creed, who sat stone face and said not a word.

As they reached the road sign for Cabarita Beach, indicating they were just a kilometer from Darlington's house, Jack reached down and turned the siren on. The following patrol cars did the same. Within minutes, the three patrol cars were double parked outside the Cypress Avenue property of Mick and Kay Darlington.

Two officers were sent to the rear of the property. Creed scaled the stairs two at a time and began banging on the front door, shouting, "Police. Open the door." His fist continued to pound on the door until he heard Darlington respond, "I'm coming." Boston-Wright remained at the bottom of the stairs, peering around at the neighbor's properties, some of which were now peeking through their blinds at all the commotion. As Mick Darlington opened the door, Boston-Wright joined Pratt and Creed inside the property.

"Good morning, Mr. Darlington. I have here a warrant for your arrest," Creed stated with confidence.

Darlington was stunned, rubbing his eyes to wake himself up. He tugged on his right ear.

"I am arresting you on the suspicion of murder for Darlene Ferguson, Tom Langley, Jessica Campbell, Sharon Berg and Sam Thompson. Creed began reading his Darlington's rights. You do not have to say anything but it may harm your defense if you do not mention when questioned something you later rely on in court. Anything you say may be given in evidence."

Darlington looked stunned. Kay Darlington stood crying uncontrollably. Mick Darlington walked into the lounge room.

"Is this a joke?" Mick Darlington asked. He looked wide-eyed as he rolled his tongue inside his dry mouth. For the first time Boston-Wright saw fear in Mick Darlington. With an outplaced arm, he asked to read the warrant. He read it for a second time before handing it back to Creed.

"Looks in order. Let me get dressed but I'll tell you something for nothing. You are making a huge mistake," Darlington remarked as he returned to the bedroom to change. Mrs. Darlington continued to cry as Boston-Wright moved in to comfort her, only to be rejected with a swift shrug of her shoulders.

Darlington appeared moments later in light brown slacks, a matching jacket with a beige long sleeve shirt under. He looked quite formal. Perhaps he was making a statement. The detectives escorted Darlington down to the patrol car, his hands cuffed in front of him. By this time there was quite a gathering of neighbors on the street, their murmurs quite audible. "Always thought he was a bit weird," said one onlooker as Mick Darlington was placed in the rear seat of Pratt's patrol car alongside Creed. Boston-Wright returned to the station with Constable Smith.

O'Halloran was visible from the second floor of the

station as the patrol cars returned. He had been updated on the imminent arrest of Darlington, giving his approval for Creed to seek the formal warrant. The station was abuzz. Interview Room 1 had been specially cleaned in waiting for Darlington's arrival.

Darlington was taken to the holding cells while his solicitor arrived. The duty Sergeant asked Darlington to remove the laces from his shoes and the belt from his trousers. His jacket was also removed, neatly folded and all items placed into a plastic bag. Darlington signed the officer's sheet, acknowledging his items.

Darlington, along with the detectives, would anxiously spend the next sixty minutes waiting for the solicitor to arrive. It felt like four hours. Creed paced in his office while Pratt downed his third cup of coffee for the morning. Boston-Wright sat back in her chair, going over her notes and occasionally looking up at Creed, who continued to pace and bite his nails.

Peter Carter finally arrived at the station, apologizing profusely about the traffic. He was ushered straight into Creed's office.

"I take it, Detective, you've got something more than the circumstantial evidence you had last time we met?" Carter commented, removing a file and notepad from his briefcase.

"Absolutely, Mr. Carter. We are wanting to chat to him about the murders in the Tweed Coast." Creed replied, pushing the case summaries over to Carter for his perusal.

"You say murders, as in plural."

"That's right. Five to be exact."

Creed sat back in his chair, keeping a watchful eye on Carter and looking for any sign his client might be in deep trouble. He wasn't disappointed. An extended raised eyebrow and a few intermittent sighs assured Creed that Carter was taking the allegations seriously. Carter asked to be shown to the cells to brief his client.

"My apologies for being late, Mick. Got held up in traffic and I've just been talking with Detective Creed," Carter said to Darlington, who returned an unimpressed look.

"Just get me out of here. I feel claustrophobic," Darlington replied, pacing the cell walls while running his hands through his hair.

"That may take some doing, Mick. They've got a decent amount of evidence," Carter responded, rubbing his chin in order to hide his unconfident look.

Creed and Pratt were already sitting in Interview Room 1 when Darlington and his solicitor walked in, escorted by Constable Smith. The smell of Dettol lingered from the spring clean that happened earlier in the morning. Creed's nosed twitched as it activated his sinuses.

The rest of the team, including Boston-Wright, hung back in the incident room. There was a deadly hush over the station. The last eighteen months of investigation and an ever-bulging budget all rested on Creed to make the evidence stick. He needed to bring his A-game today; his reputation depended on it. O'Halloran had phoned down to the team asking for hourly updates.

Smith left the room briefly and returned with a fresh pot of coffee, raspberry and white chocolate muffins and a jug of ice-cold water, placing the latter and four glasses on the interview table. She stepped back and stood guard at the door.

Pratt leaned across and turned on the recording tape and video camera, announcing all those present in the room. Darlington sat motionless, appearing to be calm although the tight clasping of his hands under the table signaled otherwise. Carter organized his pad and adjusted his spectacles as Creed took out a photo of a Nissan Patrol and placed it on the table for all to view.

"Mr. Darlington, did you own a white Nissan Patrol, registration AAF 769, up until approximately seven months ago?" Creed asked, starting the questioning.

"No, not technically. My wife did," Darlington replied coolly and succinctly. Creed glanced at Pratt, thinking the smart-ass replies had already started.

"Around that time, did you report this vehicle stolen to the Pottsville Police Station?" Creed continued.

"Yes, we did," Darlington replied, once again being short and sharp. His Army training was being recalled heavily now.

"You made out to all and sundry that the vehicle had been trashed by a gang of local aboriginal kids and you never got it back, but in fact you had sold it onto a Mr. Nicholas Finch, owner of The Bear Club in Cabarita Beach and Leather Boys in Kings Cross Sydney. Is that true?"

"Kay didn't want the car back. It was in a horrible state. Slashed back seat. Vomit on the floor. McDonald's hamburgers smeared on the internal roof lining. It was a complete mess. She was adamant that we got rid of it, so I sold it to Nick Finch. He was looking for an old knock about to go fishing in."

Creed opened the Berg folder; the photo of a strangled Sharon Berg laid front and center.

"This is Sharon Berg, an American negress, who was holidaying in Australia in September, eight months ago. She was found strangled at the rear of the Roxy Nightclub in Springwood. I put it to you, Mr. Darlington, you killed her." Creed dropped his first powerful close, teasing for a confession but knowing it was unlikely. He was hoping for some shock value, but Darlington remained cool. It was if he were meditating, keeping his heart rate low, an old Army trick used in case you were ever caught by the enemy and interrogated.

"Never been anywhere near the place. Can't stand Brisbane. It's a hole," Darlington replied.

"What is more interesting, Mr. Darlington, is that we found a piece of bubble gum wedged up under the front passenger seat," Creed continued, noticing Darlington was starting to move from side to side in his seat, crossing his legs infrequently.

"I chew gum every now and then. Good breath freshener." Darlington smiled back.

"Not sure what kind of a fresh breath tootie fruitie gum would give you, Mr. Darlington. And did I mention the brand? It's Dubble Bubble and it can only be purchased in the United States. Forensics have identified the gum is eight months old, the same time you owned the Nissan Patrol. It has Sharon Berg's DNA all over it. How do you explain that, Mr. Darlington?" Creed asked.

Darlington solicitor leaned across, grabbing his left forearm and whispering in his client's ear.

"No idea, Detective," Darlington replied, a glistening glow of perspiration now evident on his top lip.

"Come on, Mr. Darlington, we know it was you. You have a thing for colored girls and when Sharon Berg didn't want to play, you killed her and dumped her body behind the Roxy. Isn't that right?"

Darlington's shoulders slumped. He sat motionless for a few seconds while he processed the information Creed had exhibited. His eyes welled, and then he sat up straight, placed his feet flat on the floor and commented, "Is that all?"

Creed knew he had softened Darlington. He was, in boxing terms, wobbling on his feet; the tears showed that. It was time to deliver some more body blows, and then go in for the king hit. Smith motioned forward, indicating she was going to serve coffee and muffins but Creed retaliated with a death stare that stopped her in her tracks. Creed wanted Darlington to feel the pressure.

Creed opened Darlene Ferguson's file and placed it on top of Sharon Berg's.

"Darlene Ferguson, part time cleaner at the Hastings Point Caravan Park. She was killed and her body dumped in scrubland next to the park. Did you get lazy, Mr. Darlington?" Creed asked. Pratt sensed they were close and stared at Darlington, burning his soul to the core.

"What do you mean?" Darlington asked.

"We know a dead body is a dead weight. Couldn't you drag it further away?" Pratt interjected.

"I wasn't there when that poor girl was murdered," Darlington smarted.

"And so where were you, Mr. Darlington?" Pratt asked. Creed fidgeted on his seat and leaned forward. Carter prepped his client to take his time. He could sense the detectives were looking for any kind of slip up.

"I was working on a horse stud outside of Casino for a few weeks. I stayed onsite. Ask Charlie Warburton from Dad's Army. He got me the job," Darlington said gruffly, the tears returning. Pratt looked inquisitively at Creed.

"But you were seen in the area, Mr. Darlington, when Darlene Ferguson's body was found," Creed stated.

"I had just come back from the job. Kaysie had been staying in the park for a couple of weeks. She needed a break. I assume it was Finch who told you he saw me. He saw me in Woolies at Cabarita Beach. I was just getting some more groceries. I never left Casino before that. Check with Ian Brown, the property owner."

Creed leaned past Pratt and stopped both the audio and video, adjourning the interview. They walked briskly back to Creed's office, closing the door. They needed to consider Darlington's statement and check his alibi. The rest of the team looked up, hoping to get some indication as to what was going on. O'Halloran had rung down earlier but there was no news at that time.

Creed leaned back in his chair, his hands interlocked behind his head. Pratt looked concerned.

"What if his story stacks up, Jack? What if he wasn't there? What if Brown collaborates Darlington's story? We're screwed," Pratt commented, his voice crackling with dryness.

Creed tilted his chair back and forth, rubbing his hands through his hair and tugging at his face, hoping the extra blood flow would be enough stimuli to crack this case.

"But what puzzles me is that he started off cool and then he welled up a couple of times. Did you see that?" Pratt asked.

"Yes, Jim. He wasn't tearing up because he was guilty. More to the point, he had suddenly worked out who the murderer was."

"Uh?"

"We've arrested the wrong Darlington. Kay Darlington is our murderer," Creed exploded. "You go back into the interview room and keep them there. Let Mick Darlington know that I'm checking out his alibi. I'm going to take Boston-Wright and head down to Darlington's place to arrest Kay. Don't let on, though. We'll keep them separate when I return."

Creed and Boston-Wright drove like the wind down to Cabarita Beach. Creed cursed himself a few times but didn't elaborate, just saying, "How could I have missed that?" Boston-Wright asked what he had missed.

"Kay Darlington has been with Mick Darlington on most of his work trips. Casino just recently, Sydney and Pottsville. Remember he's said on a few occasions that it was Kay who had issues with aboriginals and if you throw Sharon Berg into the mix, colored people. Something to do with her upbringing in Far North Queensland." Boston-Wright acknowledged Creed was right.

Creed pulled up outside Darlington's house, carefully parking the patrol car across the driveway. Creed sprinted up the stairs with Boston-Wright following suit. He knocked on the front door. It was slightly ajar. The two officers drew their pistols as they entered the property.

"Mrs. Darlington, it's the police," Creed cried out. There was no answer. They moved down the hallway to the lounge. A leaky faucet chimed in from the kitchen. The house was eerie. A deadly silence sent a chilling air over the officers.

Boston-Wright noticed two wedding photos had been moved and now sat dominantly in the middle of the coffee table. Against the photos leaned two envelopes, one addressed to Mick Darlington the other to Detective Jack Creed.

"Sir," cried out Boston-Wright as she retrieved the letters.

"Yes, Boston-Wright, I know." Creed was solemn as he stood in the doorway of the bathroom. Kay Darlington was dead in a tub of blood-red water, her wrists slashed.

Jo handed the envelope to Creed, who read her last letter.

Dear Detective Creed,

I guessed it wouldn't take you long to figure out once you arrested my Michael this morning. The poor darling never had a clue. I just couldn't bear to see his face of disappointment.

We had a good marriage, Detective, but a loveless one. That was mainly my doing. When I was a young girl, I grew up in Cairns. I had a good life there. Every afternoon I'd catch the bus from St. Monica's into town with friends, and then another home to Earlville. But one day my life in Cairns totally changed forever.

I was raped by an aboriginal boy from the Arurukun Mission in the toilets while I waited for my bus. I got pregnant and Dr. West performed an abortion at the request of my parents. It was highly illegal back then, but I was thankful to the doctor.

So my interest in sex diminished greatly. I felt dirty, unclean. I was never forthcoming with Michael and in a sense he suffered. I loved him and he loved me, but sex was never a priority. We never had children. On the opposite scale, my hatred for aboriginals or black people in general, heightened significantly. Probably unjust, I know, but I just hated them for what Archie Thompson did to me that afternoon.

But officer, being a male yourself, men have needs. I always assumed Michael would need the pleasures of the soul at various times, but I buried the thought deep into my subconscious. This turned him to seeking this pleasure outside our marriage. It hurt, but what could I expect? I had cut off love making 20 years ago.

But my hurtfulness turned to rage when I discovered Michael was visiting prostitutes. If that wasn't bad enough, I learnt they were black prostitutes. Black – I couldn't believe it!

On one of our trips to Sydney, he would sneak off to see his 'coloured interest.' So, one day I followed him, got the name of the hooker from one of her pals, and that was the last time he ever saw Sally Carter. I thought her death might frighten him, but his appetite continued.

One day, when he was at work, I went onto the computer. He had left his Facebook page open. There was a message from Sharon Berg, some Negress he had been conversing with for months, saying she was coming out for a holiday. Once again he made up excuses as to why he had to go out. I tried to block it from my mind, but I couldn't. Then some luck was bestowed on me.

I was up visiting my sister in Rochedale. On my way back through Springwood, I noticed this buxom, big bootie Negress hitching a ride. As I slowed down, I recognized her as Sharon Berg. I couldn't believe my luck. She never got her ride back down the coast but I never knew she stuffed gum under her seat either. A bit careless on my part in not checking the car before we sold it to Nick Finch, I suppose.

Darlene Ferguson met her fate because she was known as the local 'bike' at the Hastings Point Caravan Park. Some of the regulars would snicker behind my back. It didn't take me long to put two and two together. For a slight-framed girl she was a heavy bitch. I tried to plant a seed into Michael's head that the sleaze ball Finch might be involved; that's when we dropped his name to you.

I thought I had started to control my urges against black people. I know they are not all bad. There are plenty of other folks who are pricks as well. Just look at that Tom Langley bastard. He used and abused Ferguson for years.

No, I thought I had the black thing out of my system, but Sam Thompson was my breaking point. He lived across the street. His mother was an alcoholic, no father to be seen. As a little kid he was tolerable. But when he left school, he became a total shit. Never worked a day in his life. That got my back up, both of our backs actually.

We often had to call the police on his drunken parties. It was relentless. Sometimes seven nights a week until 4am. We didn't sleep for years. Once again, I was faced with an irresponsible black person living near me, and to top it off, he had the same surname as my rapist – Thompson. I saw red everyday with that little arsehole.

One Saturday night, Michael asked me to drop him off at the Surf Club near the pub. As I swung the car around to get back onto the main road, I saw Sam walking past that gay joint the Bear Club, bumming a smoke off the bouncer.

I slowed down and glared at him. He came over to my window and gestured by putting his index finger into a circle he made with his other hand. He was indicating having sex. Cheeky bastard!

When he got home, he was straight into the booze and playing loud music. I felt trapped. This bastard was never going to leave our street. I would have to put up with this forever. I wasn't prepared to do that.

I confronted him, pushing my way into his house. His mother was away, in the nut house I think, and there he was as high as a kite, thumping out that stupid techno music kids listen to. He was in such a comatose state that he never felt me thrusting the carving knife into him. It felt good, but I wanted to make a statement with Sam Thompson. I wanted to cleanse my soul once and for all.

I went home and grabbed a hammer, a Jerry can of petrol, and the handcuffs. You saw his charred remains.

Detective Creed, I am now free of this burden that I've carried for most of my life. I have no regrets. Please pass on my love to Michael and the letter I wrote for him.

Kay Darlington

Creed folded up the letter and returned it to its envelope. He looked at Boston-Wright and shook his head. They cast their eyes around the walls and atop the television cabinet at all the happy photographs of the couple on their camping adventures.

"Photos never really tell the whole picture, do they, Boston-Wright? Happy on the outside, and so much anguish within," Creed commented as the ambulance and relieving constables arrived.

****

Greg Pratt's sendoff was a low-key affair at the Kingscliff Hotel. It was a sendoff and a celebration for the whole team on a job well done in cleaning up the Tweed Coast murders, although Mrs. Darlington's suicide dampened their spirits.

O'Halloran put a sizeable tab on the bar and thanked Pratt for his 27 years of service to the force. Cara Pratt and their two sons cheered on the man who had contributed so much to policing in their area and now finally they would have him at home to themselves.

Creed stood at the back, raising his glass and cheering on the well-wishers as they lined up to say a few good words about Detective Greg Pratt. Boston-Wright sidled up to Creed.

"A big loss, sir."

"Yes, I'll miss him. He's given his best, and it's only fair we hand him back to his family now." Creed looked through the crowd to Mrs. Pratt, who was beaming with pride.

"But all is not lost, Jo. I've got you to step up now. You did well on this case. You are every bit as good as your father. Here's to our future." He clinked his glass with Boston-Wright's.

ABOUT THE AUTHOR

C T Mitchell is an Australian mystery fiction author of fast paced, impossible to put down, maximum entertainment short reads that can be devoured in your lunch hour or on your train ride home after work. Sometimes he goes all out by writing a thrilling full-length novel; something you shouldn't read at night.

His books can be read as individual reads, in any order within several different traditional detective and cozy mystery series. Readers rate them 4.1/5 on average

Detective Jack Creed, D S Jo Boston-Wright, Lady Margaret Turnbull, Kate Mackenzie, Father Douglas and Selena Sharma are C T Mitchell's much loved characters; many of whom you can discover on the Book Characters page on his website.

Start your C T Mitchell Library with two free mystery novels bestsellers when you subscribe to his newsletter on his site. (unsubscribe at any time)

Contact C T Mitchell
Website: http://www.CTMitchellBooks.com
http://www.TheShortReads.com

Facebook:

http://www.facebook.com/CTMitchellAuthor

http://www.facebook.com/theshortreads

Twitter: http://www.twitter.com/theshortreads

FREE Downloads

Grab 2 FREE #1 Amazon eBooks at

www.FreeCrimeBooks.com

BOOK REVIEWS

Can I ask for your help?

I love writing. I aim to entertain you. While I'll never win the Nobel Prize for Literature, I am a student of personal development on a continual journey to improve my writing and partner with the best book cover designers, proofreaders, editors, publishers and book promoters.

As a self-publishing indie author, I rely on you to become part of my Reader's Group by growing your C T Mitchell library. If you liked what you read today, could I ask you to leave a positive review? Book reviews can make or break a book and ultimately affect the income of an author.

But…..

Not everybody will love my work. Even though this book has been professionally edited twice, proofread and spell checked, mistakes still can occur. We all make them. If you've found something incorrect or wanted to offer some suggestions to improve this and my future books, please email me at:

cabaritacrimes@gmail.com

Thank you again for reading my book. It means the world to me. I hope you'll leave a positive review.

C T Mitchell

www.ingramcontent.com/pod-product-compliance
Lightning Source LLC
Chambersburg PA
CBHW050157120726
47903CB00002B/660